Barbarian

Tales

Books 1, 2 & 3

www.BarbarianSpy.com

This book is copyright © Sabb 2010
First published by BarbarianSpy in 2010.
Cover design by S Bush © 2010
Cover Photos S Bush © 2010
All rights reserved
ISBN Ebook 978-0-9808490-9-7
ISBN Print 978-1-921879-20-3

Published by BarbarianSpy an imprint of Cyberworld Publishing
Jindalee St, Toronto, Australia.

BarbarianSpy

Not all books listed below may currently be on release.

BOOKS BY SABB

Surprise Encounters
She is He
Wrong Man
Loyal to his King
Barbarian Tales - Book One - Traveller's Tales
Barbarian Tales - Book Two - Journeys Begin
Barbarian Tales - Book Three - The Inheritance
Barbarian Tales - Book Four - Road to Persepolis

BOOKS BY SHABBU

Cigars!
Angel in the Barn
Gayly Complicated
Despoiling David
Tree of Idleness
Rough Road to Happiness
I Met a Man
The Interview

BOOKS BY HABU

Journey to Mirage
Cairo Surrender
Fetish Galore!
Homeward Bound

BOOKS BY DIRK HESSIAN

Prophecy of Noto
The King's Men
Labyrinth

BARBARIAN TALES

Book 1 Traveler's Tales

Book 2 Journeys Begin

Book 3 The Inheritance

SABB

CONTENTS

Book 1

Traveler's Tales

CONTENTS

Introduction

Many men talk of Konan the great barbarian with wonder and awe, and some lucky few have true tales to tell of him. Of the time they crossed the path of that great giant of a man, and if they are very lucky, they talk too, with faraway eyes, of being taken by him and of the power of his taking. And occasionally Konan has told his own tale, a tale of some man who pleased him greatly.

In his journeys, Konan has met many men, and these are the tales of some of them.

Tales of simple travelers, of young barbarians of the tribe of Urk who were kidnapped and rescued. Of merchants who met him on the road and whom he traveled with as a caravan guard, of men he saved using his sexual prowess and his cunning. And of men he loved.

These tales are also told by those whom Konan, the Great Barbarian, met when in the land of the Great Mogul, which lies far to the west of where Konan began his life, and far to the west of where we all live. These are the tales of those he knew when he was a captive of the Great Mogul's grand general, and tales of the fine young nobleman who came to court to make his fortune and of the great general's son, the young prince Kasim, and of how, by saving Kasim, Konan gained his freedom to continue his journey through the ancient world.

Through these men's stories and his own, Konan shares his history with you.

I Meet a Barbarian

He came over the dusty hilltop and walked down the road toward me. As he came closer, my mouth fell open. I had never before seen such a massive muscular physique. His arms tapered from massive shoulders to thick-boned wrists and big, strong hands. His legs . . . well, his legs were huge, his massive thighs a moving mass of rippling muscle as he strode smoothly toward me. He wore only a calfskin loincloth and some leather straps about his chest. The loincloth covered his crotch, but as he moved, it flapped back and forth, and I could see that it was never going to hang straight down on him. There was far too much of a mound sitting behind it for that.

As he strode closer, he looked me over. It was a direct assessment of my physical attributes. "Where are you from?" I shouted to him, as he got close enough to hear.

"Why do you ask?" he bellowed back.

"I have never seen a man who looked as muscular and strong as you do," I replied, not wanting to offend him but unable to stop looking down at that loincloth of his, trying to figure out just what was behind it.

He laughed as he reached me. "I have had a long walk and need to rest a while. Do you want join me?" he asked.

I gulped, "yes, of course, I have a water skin you can drink from too," I replied, taking up the leading rein on my donkey, which carried my provisions. "Umm, where do you want to rest?"

He indicated a pile of huge rocks that stood beside the road. "There."

I smiled, seeing that the rocks made some cool shade. I stepped off toward them, but he landed a huge hand on my ass and grabbed a handful of my dusty tunic. He spun me around, and his huge arms pulled me in to him, and he planted his lips on mine, crushing them. His hands were on my ass, each huge hand almost completely enclosing a cheek.

"Ummm," he grunted, as he let me fall free.

I could see his loin cloth was standing out more now than before, and I was transfixed by the obvious bulge now being made by what was behind it.

"Come on," he said, taking my arm in a powerful and almost painful grasp.

Once we reached the shade of the rocks, he pushed me back against the nearest. I gasped and was a bit worried for a moment; then he removed his loincloth, and I was too stunned by what was revealed to worry about anything else. What he had been hiding was a huge engorging cock, already more than one span long, and big, sagging balls. He stroked his cock, which was still only partly hard but already as thick and long as any I had seen before.

"Do you have any oil?" he asked.

I nodded numbly, "In the pack on my donkey's side," I replied.

"Get it," he ordered me.

I scurried over to my pack animal and dug out the clay jar of cooking oil and returned to hand it to him. He pushed me about, and I ended up facing the rock with him behind me. I had a pretty good idea where this was going.

He slapped a huge hand on my shoulder and pulled my tunic down, tearing it off me. Then I felt huge fingers parting my cheeks and his hand slapped oil onto my ass. It dribbled down my thighs as he pulled my hips away from the rock, and my legs followed, until I was supporting only my head with my hands against the rock. He slathered more oil onto my ass, and then I cried out, "OOOH," as he plunged one of his thick fingers into my asshole.

My ass was a well-used piece of equipment, but it had never served a man built like he was. I turned my head as far as I could and gasped fearfully when I saw the huge rod he now stroked with his free hand. "I don't—" I began, my protest cut off by him jamming a thicker finger deep inside me.

He stroked the head of his huge cock against my hole, wetting me more and spreading the slippery oil about on himself as well as me. I cried out as something burned its way inside me. He laughed. My ass was emptied and I wanted it filled, but I wasn't sure if what he was offering me was going to be able to be accommodated inside there.

He was not concerned though, and in a moment, I was screaming a scream that echoed through the pile of rocks and across the valley. He had got inside me. His huge cock was tearing my entrance up as he eased it into me. I pushed back, trying to make my ass open wider, putting my hands back to pull my own cheeks apart. He continued to drive himself into me, and I continued to let out screams of agony.

But then he had hit that spot, and I was gasping for breath between my screams. The oil and my body were suddenly helping him ease in, and he was making way inside me without tearing me apart. I groaned now with huge groans and crying moans. He was going deeper than I'd known a cock could go and stretching me to my limit and almost beyond, but he kept going. Then he was in. I gasped and panted, sweating with the strain of taking him.

He grunted too, and his cock moved inside me, and I screamed again. Then he slapped my ass hard and started to fuck me with small bumps of his great hips. They bumped my ass so hard they nearly drove my head into the rock I was leaning against. His bumping became fiercer, and my wails again echoed through the valley.

He grunted again and suddenly pulled out of me. I nearly collapsed onto the hard ground but he pushed me back to the rock and turned me about. I was shaking still from the strain of his fucking me, and he handled me like a soft toy.

He bent down and lifted my legs off the ground, and I yelled out as he pushed my back up the rock behind me and locked my bent knees over his forearms and spread them as wide as he could.

My asshole was now ideally placed for him, and I gasped fearfully as I saw his engorged cock was now well over a span and a half in length. It stood out so hard he just pulled me forward so my ass rode down on it. I screamed again as I felt it going into me, deeper than before, if that was possible. It was slightly easier for me to take spread wide as I was, but now my back was being rubbed raw by the rough rock behind me.

The he pushed me effortlessly off his cock to near the end of it. I was no more than a bag of straw to his huge muscles. Then he pulled me in again, his cock plunging back deep in me, while I screamed a piercing scream. He ignored my protests and built up a steady fucking rhythm with his hips and my body.

It was all I could do not to faint as he plowed my ass like that. He kept the pushing-pulling fuck up for some time. Then I felt him twitch inside me, making me scream again, while he plunged deep, threw his head back, and roared like a lion. There was a great surge of warmth inside me. He roared again, and I felt another flood fill me. I came myself, over my belly and chest, just from the feel of him coming inside me.

Then his cum began to run out of me and dribble down his thighs. He pushed me off him finally, and my legs refused to hold me up. I collapsed into a heap at the base of the rock that had rubbed my back raw. I couldn't move and wondered if I'd ever walk again.

He smiled down at me while he replaced his loincloth. When he was done, he said to me, "Well met stranger," and, waving me farewell, he turned away and returned to the road, striding off into the distance as I lay on the ground, totally fucked and drifting off into unconsciousness.

I awoke to the cold of nighttime and wondered why I was lying there and wondered too at the odd dream I'd had of being fucked by a giant. Then I moved, and the pain it caused me told me it had been no dream. I certainly had been fucked by a giant. And I knew too that my poor donkey was going to be unhappy at having to carry me on his back the next day, as my ass was going to be unhappy sitting astride his hard back. But I doubted I would walk properly for some time.

Barbarian Surprise

I lay on the ground where I had been thrown, panting for air, and looking up at a giant of a man who stood over me. He was muscular and solid with large legs and thighs like tree trunks, narrow hips covered by nothing but a hide loincloth, and above that a belly that consisted of waves of muscle and then a chest—a huge chest with big nipples rimmed by golden hair—that was joined to arms that bulged. The golden hair ran down his belly to the leather of his loincloth and spread over his legs.

He laughed down at me and poked his sharply pointed sword at my manhood. I reached to protect myself but, the flat of the sword slapped my hand free, and with a twist of his wrist, he had sliced open the fine fabric of my pants, and my manhood was exposed.

He smiled down at me and tapped at my stiffening cock with his sword, and I moaned. Then he sliced and flicked away the rest of my pants, then began to work on my fine linen shirt, and in mere moments I lay there naked beneath him.

I wondered wildly, "How, how have I come to this?"

I had been minding my own business, resting in my tent, reclining on a pile of rugs and pillows as my men repacked the wagons. We had passed through a heavy storm the day before, and water had penetrated through some of the skins and waxed linen wrappings that covered the more valuable items in my load of merchandise.

This was my first trading trip alone, and we had crossed the plains in very good time and were about to make our way into the foothills, and I wanted nothing spoiled. The dangerous part of our journey was over, and we had not been troubled by bandits. I was feeling pleased and relaxed, and as I listened to the low sound of the men talking and working outside, I was stroking myself, thinking of the fleshpots of Tamarind that we would reach in another two days.

"Ahh," I sighed, as thoughts of nubile young men and women filled my head.

On previous visits to the city, my time in the brothels had been limited by the presence of my father and his need to always hurry. He was a very serious man who thought of nothing but business and spent all his time trading or cultivating useful contacts. We barely stopped in Tamarind for one night when he was in charge.

I knew that I would never be like that. "No," I sighed, "there is more to life than business," and I planned on spending at least two days in that wonderful city of pleasure, perhaps more, and I remembered a particularly beautiful . . .

There was a thud against the wall of my tent, and I frowned, distracted from my happy fantasy. Then there was a yelp, and I was suddenly alert and annoyed. My men were well disciplined, and if there was a fight I would deal harshly with the men involved. And now my mood was spoiled; I called my foreman in.

"Marco," I called.

I expected an instant response from him, but nothing happened. I waited and, "Marco," I shouted again, angrily and loudly.

Still nothing. Suddenly my tent felt like a trap that blinded me to what was happening outside it, and I was worried. I lay there undecided. No one had bothered me yet, so perhaps if I just stayed quiet. But no, that was a truly unworthy thought. So I stood up and crept quietly to the tent's entrance and turned the fabric aside just enough to look out.

Everything outside seemed normal, except that there was no one about. Wagons stood half loaded, horses grazed on their tethers. All was quiet. It was most odd.

I tiptoed back to where my sword hung from the central pole of the tent and drew it quietly, then returned to the entrance.

"I must do this," I said silently and opened the flap.

But there was no longer nothing outside. A huge hand grabbed the wrist of my sword arm and twisted it painfully till my sword had fallen to the ground, to be swept up and away by someone I could not see, as the body of some huge giant filled my sight.

He held my wrist and jerked me out of the tent and tossed me to the ground where I landed on my back.

And now I lay there naked and wondering fearfully what he intended to do with me. My breathing quickly growing more rapid as his eyes traveled over my body and his sword stayed hovering over my jewels.

Then he reached down and pulled me up and propelled me back into the tent.

"Who are you? What do you want of me?" I cried out to him, suddenly finding my voice at last, as I staggered across the tent before falling to my knees among the rugs by the thick central pole of the tent. "My father . . ." I began, but he cut me off.

"It is not often that a fine healthy young man, such as you, comes my way," he told me in the rough accents of a barbarian, as he tied my hands together with some leather thong, making me even more helpless. Then he pulled me up by the arms to a standing position, and turning me, he tied the cord at my wrists to the top of the pole, so I was stretched out and naked there.

I was panting fearfully and hating my cock for bouncing against my belly at full attention.

Once I was helpless, he fisted my tool several times, till I groaned and moved my hips for him, then he laughed and came to in front of me and dropped his loincloth. I gasped and felt faint; while he smiled and wrapped his hand about the largest erect phallus I had ever seen and worked it to an even greater hardness.

"This I have in my hand is for you, my young merchant," he told me before he disappeared behind me, and I scrabbled my legs about, and writhed, trying to escape, but also trying to widen myself for the imminent attack.

"Oh. No," I gasped, "You can't. I've never . . . 'it's impossible. You will kill me," I wailed as huge hands parted my cheeks and pulled at my rim. "No, no."

But then it was a wet warm tongue of good size that was there, softly working my rim and pushing in and out of me, and I went weak and moaned and lifted a leg high, giving him better access. His huge tongue worked in me as few but the best in the brothels had. Ahhh, it was inside moving; ahhh, it was better tongue work than in any brothel.

"Yessss," I moaned, "Oh, no. Oh, yes."

His tongue played inside my channel as his hands squeezed my cheeks and traveled briefly to my balls to play there a moment, then to stroke my hard, dripping cock. I was confused enough to beg him for more. Though visions of that huge phallus, which I doubted both my hands could cover, and his large hairy balls that I doubted I could take more than one of in my mouth at any time, filled my head, and I whimpered.

"Ohhh. No," I moaned as the tongue left me. But something thick and hard replaced it in my channel, going deeper and rotating and . . . "Oh gods," I cried lifting my legs and wrapping them about the pole to open myself as another thick long finger joined the first inside me. They were stretching and teasing my channel so my hips fucked instinctively and my manhood rubbed against the tent pole, and in a moment I spouted my load of seed up my chest and over the pole.

I was spent then and sagged back onto the fingers digging inside me, and a firm hand grasped one cheek and held me up, so that my shoulders were not strained by carrying my full weight. My head dropped back, and full lips found mine, and a tongue explored my mouth.

He ended the kiss and grunted, "Now you will feel the manhood of Konan," to me, and I whimpered even before the bulbous head of his weapon pressed against my entrance.

I cried out loudly as he forced it past the first resistance, and I strained to open myself for him. He gained another inch, and he had a mighty palm under each of my cheeks and lifted me and opened me wider, and I moaned as he gained another inch. Then he was lowering me onto his mighty tool, and I whimpered, "I can't. Oh, I . . . Ohhhhh." He had reached that spot. "Ohhhhh," I moaned, and I felt myself open for him so that he moved in deeper.

There was some pain, but my channel was not a virgin one and opened for him slowly but steadily, and finally he was buried to the hilt in me, and I could feel that thick golden hair of his bush brushing against my hairless butt. And a fullness filled me inside such as I had never felt before.

Then he plowed me deep, the strength of his thrusting lifting me up the pole and then powering up into me as I was let down, and turning me about it and moving himself in circles in me so that I moaned and cried out, "Yes. Oh, great Gods, again. Ride me. Oh, never have I, oh . . ." and similar cries of ecstasy at being so well ridden.

But all too soon he began to pump me rapidly and swell, and I cried out at the even bigger size of him splitting me as he let loose, pumping his first shot of seed deep inside me. And as he did, he let out a great roar, like a lion, that sent a shiver through my body, and I shot another load of my own up the pole, which my legs still embraced, as he deposited even more of his man-juice deep inside me with another great roar of power and strength.

When he finally withdrew from me, I collapsed and felt his cream run out of me as I wondered if I might tear my shoulders from hanging there, too weak to stand on my shaking legs. The cream ran down my inner thighs, and the cord at my wrists was sliced free and I collapsed to the ground, whimpering.

"You have given me a fine ride, young merchant," He said in his deep rough voice. "But be warned that if you return here within the five days that remain before I return to my winter home, I shall ride you again, and ride you even harder."

With that he was gone.

As I lay there recovering myself enough so I could stand again, I heard soft murmurings coming from outside and the normal sounds of the day returned. Eventually, I left my tent to find the wagons almost ready and Marco helping to secure the horses in their traces, and I had barely left my tent when men hurried to dismantle it and I was still in a daze when it was packed up on top of the last wagon, which held our own food and possessions.

Marco came up to me, "We are ready to leave master," he said looking at me normally.

"Good," I said, pulling my wits together and walking carefully to the last wagon. "I will ride up here for now," I told him, gingerly climbing up and setting myself down onto a thick cushion that was unexpectedly placed on the seat up there. "I will ride Hercules (my horse) later. And, Marco, I wish us to make good speed to Tamarind and tell the men there will be no delays there. I wish us to leave for our return journey within the day."

Marco looked up at me, now smiling very broadly, and replied, "Just as your great father would wish, master. He is indeed the smartest merchant in all of Thrace," he added, and I wondered why he seemed so cheerful and pleased.

Then I wondered where he had been when the barbarian had knocked me down and dragged me into my tent.

Hum. Perhaps I should not wonder too much on such things.

Barbarian Initiation

Throwing his head back and arching his body, Garr cried to his lover in ecstasy, "Deeper, deeper," and wrapped his legs about the barbarian Konan's narrow hips, pulling their pelvises even closer and more tightly together, as the barbarian plowed the lean young mountain warrior's ass canal with his huge weapon.

And he was plowing the lean young warrior Garr very well, and very deeply and fully, for he was Konan. And Garr lay back and bucked his hips for him as he did. Then Konan plowed him for a long time more as Garr ran his legs up his lover's chest and Konan pulled his thighs in close. And Garr moaned and cried out in his passion, "Ride me hard, barbarian, work my ass with your mighty tool; never stop. Oh, deeper. Oh faster. Ohh. Fillllll meeeee," he cried as he shuddered and released his own pent-up cream, so it shot up his belly to his chest and beyond.

But it had not always been so. When they had met, Garr had been full of fear of Konan's mighty weapon. And his fears were understandable, unfortunately, for Garr had been cruelly treated when a captive of the raiders who had taken him and were known to be slave traders. And the great barbarian Konan had shown another side of himself to free Garr of his fear.

* * * *

Urk and Konan were crouched down and watching.

The raiders' camp looked to have been occupied for some time, with a pen set up for their horses and many possessions in piles lying under the rock. It was set up on smooth sand that lay in the shadow of a great stone overhang on the bank of the river. Its bed was mostly sand now in the dry season, but there was a narrow channel of fast-flowing water at its center, and odd marshy patches could be seen in the distance, in the wider river bed. The smoke of the raider's small campfire was being broken up and dispersed by the rock above them, so they could be warm and could eat cooked meat without giving any sign of their hiding place to those searching for them. And it had only been Urk's great skill as a tracker that had brought him and Konan to this hidden, secret place.

Now, as evening fell, the friends were hidden behind huge slabs of rock that had fallen eons ago from the cliffs above them, and were observing the rituals of the camp. And they smelt the aroma of grilling meat, which reminded them that their own stomachs were empty and rumbling after two full days of searching.

They watched the dozen dark-haired raiders sitting about their fire, eating grilled meat and passing a wine skin between themselves, laughing and talking. This continued for some time until it was fully dark and the only light was from the fire and from the moon that hung conveniently low in the sky above the far bank of the riverbed. When the food was eaten and the wine almost gone, two men got up and went deeper into the shadowed space under the overhang. Konan and Urk strained to see where they had gone, but they saw no more then the two returning minutes later with a struggling captive.

Urk's body tensed at the arrival of the young mountain warrior among his captors but then relaxed partly when he saw that it was not Rogg. But it was still a young man of great importance to him, as all four of those taken by the raiders were close kin to him.

The three young warriors, and the younger, almost-warrior, Garr, had been captured when they had gone out to perform the sacred rites of initiation into manhood for Garr. And Urk and Konan both knew that the raiders would sell the four as slaves and at a good price, if they got them across the mountains and down to the great city by the sea.

Young Garr, the youngest of the four, being hardly past his eighteenth year, was the one who had been dragged out first to stand before his captors. They had formed themselves into a circle and now one from the circle stood up and went over to him, and the two watchers knew this must be the raider's leader, as he was larger than the others and wore a great collar of beads and metal about his neck, which had not been visible when he was seated on the far side of the fire. The leader examined Garr all over, inspecting his teeth, feeling his arms and legs, then tearing his loincloth away and weighing his male parts in his hands and fondling them. Urk and Konan looked on, wanting to save Garr from the humiliation he was suffering, but knowing that the two of them, even though both great warriors, could not overcome those twelve rough and dangerous raiders while they were all together.

The leader then seemed to be stroking Garr's manhood with his fist, and Garr struggled against his captors. But he was tied at the wrists and hobbled at the ankles, with one man holding his arms behind him and two others taking his legs and holding them steady and parted. So he was unable to pull his rising organ from the leader's grasp.

In the firelight Garr's pole grew to a reasonable length and thickness, and once the leader had made it spout its youthful seed, he released the young captive, who was dragged back under the rock overhang into the darkness from where he had come. Then the other three captives were dragged out one by one, and the leader examined them in a similar way. He made each one's manhood reach its full size and shoot its load before they were returned to where they had been brought from. The last to appear was Rogg, and when the leader had begun to work him up, his men all craned their necks to see the huge size and thickness of Rogg's growing organ.

As his manhood grew to its full size and thickness, Rogg was fondled by all the party, the laughing men running their hands over his balls, squeezing and tugging at them, and over his manhood, gripping it and poking at its small hole. Then one of the raiders was on his knees before him, taking that great tool into his mouth and sucking upon it greedily. And another had gone on his knees behind Rogg and had buried his face between his full muscular cheeks.

Rogg was young, and in spite of his situation, soon shook and moaned and filled the raider's mouth with his first seed, then another burst went over the man's body and a third over the hands of several. They exclaimed at the large amount of man cream Rogg had, and how strongly he pumped it out. While Urk trembled with anger at seeing them treat Rogg like some pleasure slave.

Rogg was taken away soon after, but the young lean Garr was brought out again, and Konan observed that he was not only the youngest but also the most lithe and slender of the four captives.

Now the leader had Garr pushed onto his knees, and though the young man yelled and kicked, his tied hands and his tied ankles made him helpless. Men pulled his legs as far apart as his bonds allowed and forced his head to the ground. Meanwhile, the leader pulled his short thick organ free of his own calfskin britches and waved it about and, kneeling behind the young captive, slapped it on Garr's pale ass cheeks.

Then with little preparation, he drove it into Garr's virgin hole. The young man screaming at the pain of the leader's cruel invasion. But the raiders laughed loudly, enjoying the young captive's pain, and their leader roughly and cruelly thrust into him again and again, finally spouting his seed across Garr's back as the young man fell to the ground.

Garr remained lying in a heap as the leader strutted about holding his tool, which still had some stiffness, shaking it and saying, "See how great and strong my weapon is. It has almost killed this weak mountain man. A warrior? Ha. A weakling. As are all mountain men. Fit for nothing but the slave market."

Garr was dragged away then and, to the watchers, that appeared to be the end of the evening's entertainment. The raiders moved away from the fire, or pulled their blankets closer to it, and lay down and quietened. The fire was damped down with sand till it was only a small glow, and just one man remained sitting by it and keeping watch.

The raiders had grown complacent after using the hiding place so long, and the watchman didn't wake anyone to take his place when he wandered off to piss. So they were unaware he never returned. But Konan crept back to where Urk was hidden and, squeezing his arm in reassurance, handed him another knife, the raider's blade, that was sharp and long.

Then silently Konan and Urk left their hiding spot and approached the sleeping party. The men moved under their blankets and made sleeping noises, and it was not as dark beneath the overhang as it might have been, as the moon was still sitting low in the sky. Then Urk was squatting beside one dark sleeping shape and there was no more than a faint grunt as he found a use for the raider's knife. Then he was beside another, and Konan had silently slit the throat of a third man already. Silently and quickly Urk and Konan continued their work, and there were but three or four men left alive when one turned over at the sound of a stifled cry and shouted out.

But it was too late. Those left alive were still struggling to stand as Konan and Urk reached them. The camp was suddenly silent again and Urk bent to stir the coals, throwing light over the scene of death about them. Then he threw more wood on the fire before he took up a burning log and he and Konan moved to the back of the overhang where the prisoners had been dragged.

They crawled back as the roof got lower and then found a side cave where it opened out again and the captives were in there, tied up and chained to stakes driven into the stone walls. Garr lay huddled up, his face stained with tears, and with blood—but only a small amount, the two men were

28

relieved to see—about his rear and between his thighs. Konan cut him free and almost carried him from the cave, as Urk freed the other three young men, embracing Rogg, who kissed him ferociously.

They gathered down by the flowing water in the riverbed, and though it was cold, the freed captives all lay or sat in the cleansing water. They splashed it over themselves, washing the stench of their captivity and the raider's foul hands from their lean, strong bodies.

Urk joined his lover, Rogg, in the fast-flowing water and used his hands to cleanse his lover's manhood as it quickly rose up to greet him. Then he and Rogg lay in the water and rolled about in it, embracing and cleansing themselves in the coolness, as they moved against the sand and each other. The water was cold, so they felt the heat of each other's bodies gladly and pressed against each other, with the heat of the others skin against their skin inflaming their desire even more, as they kissed and touched each other's organs and entrances.

Soon Rogg was kneeling in the water with Urk knelt behind him between his spread thighs, and Urk was running his tongue and fingers about Rogg's puckered rim as Rogg moaned and whispered to Urk of what he wanted him to do to reassert his possession of him. They were rough words of fucking and cum. And Urk had his fingers inside Rogg, as Rogg stroked his own massive pole and it spouted into the water beneath him, his seed carried off to the ocean.

Urk's own manhood was of just as massive a size as Rogg's and was standing tall and dark in the dim light, unseen precum dribbling from its tiny mouth, and Urk rubbed it over Rogg's rim and into his loosening hole.

Garr had gone a bit away from the others and lay alone in the cold water, shaking and trying to clean the stench and abuse of the raiders from his body, as Konan kept a worried eye on him. The other two young men now sat on the wet sand beside the river and, with their own tools in their hands, stroked themselves and ran their hands over their bodies, tweaking and pinching and fondling their balls, as Urk pressed the huge knob of his manhood to the loosened hole of the begging Rogg.

Rogg moaned, "Fill me. I need your manhood inside me. Drive it in. Hard. Fuck me deep. Take me, Urk. Take me strong and hard, make me yours again." And Urk did, driving his knob into Rogg's passage and then driving his tool further into him, reaching the spot he knew and rubbing his knob against that, twisting and turning it inside his lover. Then pushing his manhood deeper, Rogg welcoming it into his core with moans and cries of passion as they were connected, curling pubic hair mixed with curling ass hair, two bodies joined in shared heat and lust. Urk rocked himself inside the tight, embracing passage of his lover and moaned at the feel of that channel on his throbbing tool, as Rogg moaned with him.

There were cries of, "Yes, yes," and, "Fuck him, fuck him deep," from the two young men watching, who came quickly at the sight of Urk's great tool being buried to the hilt and then fucking in and out of Rogg's hole.

Garr blocked his ears and hissed, "How can they? It is so painful. How could any man?" and Konan heard him and replied.

"The raider was cruel. A real man will seek to give pleasure to another he enters, as Urk and Rogg do. It is a most pleasurable thing."

"I can't believe it," Garr whimpered, still trying to cleanse the suffering of his capture from his body, but unable to remove it from his mind with the cold water.

Konan soon pulled Garr from the water and half dragged him back to the fire, where he found clean rugs and wrapped them about him and fed him from what food there was about, making him eat. In the background, the sounds of Urk and Rogg's passionate joining filled the night air.

The other two young men joined them and ate their fill too and talked of their capture as Konan listened. Garr sat huddled still and joined in occasionally but said little. Konan sat closer to him and rubbed the blanket over him, as he still shivered, and young Treg asked what had happened when they took him out of the cave the second time.

"The leader forced his manhood into me," he whispered.

"So was it pleasurable?" Treg asked

"Pleasurable?" Garr cried out unexpectedly. "I cannot believe any man would find it pleasurable," he replied in anguish, showing how much he had been hurt.

Konan took hold of him and pulled him to him. "It is pleasurable for any man who is prepared well," he said firmly, looking Garr in the eyes.

"Yes," said Treg, "Konan is right," and he approached the two of them.

Konan began to run his hands over Garr's body, rubbing the lean and frightened young Garr's nipples, gently but firmly.

"See, is this not good?" the barbarian asked softly.

"Yes. But . . . but that is not what he did," Garr replied, "I . . ."

Konan found Garr's lips with his, blocking off whatever he was going to say and continued his rubbing with one hand as the other began to roam gently over Garr's body.

Treg could see Garr's nipples harden and said, "See? Is that not pleasant? You shall have your initiation now, Garr. Konan and I shall show you what you can enjoy. Remember I am kin, Garr, and would not lie to you."

"Yes. But . . ." Garr whimpered, even as his own organ began to grow under the attentions of Konan's fingers, which now gently stroked it and played with his foreskin, moving it back and revealing the head of his stiffening cock.

Then suddenly Garr tried again to pull away, because he had looked down and seen the huge tent Konan's rising manhood was making in his loincloth. Showing Garr that he was far longer, and thicker than the raider's leader had been, and frightening him.

Konan placed a great hand under Garr's chin and, lifting his face and looking into his eyes, said, "I promise that you shall feel only what is good. And my weapon is not for you, unless you ask for it."

"Never," Garr cried out, meaning it.

Kneeling behind him Treg kissed the back of Garr's neck and across his shoulders and played his hands over the younger man's back and arms, moving in and placing his thighs outside Garr's. And Konan continued to look into Garr's eyes while stroking his young manhood into hardness and occasionally let his fingers roam to Garr's sac to squeeze and tug at that.

Garr began to pant and to feel his lust rise, discovering that the attentions of the two men were bringing him to a state of heat and desire that he had never felt before. Without thought, he lifted his hips higher, raising his butt up, and Treg ran his hands under Garr's cheeks, squeezing them and stroking them and his fingers drifted closer to Garr's entrance. Now the fourth young captive, Tor, went over to them with a pot of oil that the raiders had left by the fire, and Treg and Konan dipped their fingers into it, and now Konan's hand was slick and slid over Garr's pole like silk, but tight-wrapped, caressing silk.

"Unhhh," Garr moaned, and gazing into his eyes, Konan saw him letting go of his fear.

Behind him, Treg was running oily fingers up and down the younger man's crease, sliding over his sore rim, making the hole twitch and tighten in a most pleasurable way. But Garr's eyes opened wider, looking at Konan with new fear.

"No," he whimpered, "No," moving his hands as if to push Treg and Konan away, but Konan bent his head and took Garr's mouth into a kiss and tightened the fist he was sliding up and down his pole, leaving his thumb to circle and press on the tiny mouth in it's head.

Garr lay between surrender and fright as Treg pressed the tip of one finger against Garr's twitching puckered rim, and the long slender oiled finger slid in easily. Treg closed his eyes the better to feel the place inside Garr where he wanted to rest his fingertip. Garr hung there, wondering at how easily and painlessly he had been entered this time and then was feeling something stirring deep inside him that was making his weapon leak its creamy seed. Konan felt Garr relax again and, freeing his mouth, bent his head to lick the drops from the crown of the young man's manhood.

Now Garr moaned and moved his hips in ecstasy, his hands moving to Konan's head and gripping his hair. And if there was soreness at his entrance, then he was no longer aware of it as his organ throbbed and his balls ached with the need to cum. But now Konan pulled his head back and, instead, kissed up Garr's belly to his chest and beyond to his neck, Garr moaning, "Finish me, don't stop," and reaching for his own tool but having his hands pulled away by Tor, who held them up as he kissed Garr's mouth.

Meanwhile, Treg had inserted another oily finger into Garr's passage and began to slide both in and out. Garr now moaned steadily, and his hips moved along with the action of Treg's fingers, straining too to rub his tool against Konan's great thighs, desperate to gain release.

Urk and Rogg arrived to see them thus. Garr on his knees, his thighs wide, his high as Konan crouched before him, fondling his chest and now, again, dropping his head to Garr's manhood and taking it fully into his mouth and sucking. Sucking, searching all about it with his tongue. Garr finally came, sending his spoutings once, twice, three times into Konan's throat.

Garr went weak and sagged forward then, spent, but Treg held his hips as Tor released his arms and mouth and Konan guided the young warrior's head into his lap.

Konan ran his hands over Garr's back and his ass cheeks, and as Treg withdrew his two fingers, Konan pressed just one deep into Garr's channel, stretching it more, and Garr moaned in willing acceptance. Tor looked on, stroking himself to his own release.

Treg's weapon was long and thin and already hard enough to press into Garr's loosened, well-oiled entrance, as Konan held his cheeks spread. Now Garr whimpered briefly as

Treg entered him, and again as he slid deeper and pulled back slightly, but Treg was gentle as he began to plow Garr's passage, and Garr's whimpers turned to grunts and moans of pleasure as Treg began to plow him deeply. And Garr's mouth had found the head of Konan's great weapon, and his hands reached under and pushed away the loincloth covering it, and Garr took its great cap into his mouth and began to suck and lick it greedily. And as he felt it grow to its full hardness, he couldn't stop wondering what such a massive shaft of manhood would feel like working him where Treg's fine long tool now was. And the motion of his hips grew wilder as he thought of it.

The Young Warrior Is Captured

The young warrior lay on the ground beneath the point of my sword. His breath came in ragged gasps that showed his exhaustion after our fierce struggle and racked his muscular athletic body. His eyes begged me to spare his life. But he was too proud to speak, waiting bravely for me to run my sword through him and finish the job of defeating him.

I looked him over, impressed by the rippling muscles of his heaving stomach and noting the shape of his weapon, barely hidden by the ragged and sweat soaked clothing that covered him. I pulled a long dagger from my belt and held that pointed at my captive as I sheathed my sword. Then I pulled a leather cord from my waist and, bending down, I brought his hands close together and wrapped the cord firmly about his wrists. He looked up at me with some fear, at what I might have planned for him, but also with some relief at still being alive. I tied a second leather thong loosely about his ankles, giving him enough length to walk with if he took short steps.

Then I pulled his ragged and sweat soaked loincloth down and took his partly full weapon in my hand to feel its weight and examine it more closely. I pushed back his sheath to reveal the head and thumbed his soft slit. I grunted, satisfied, but he was wriggling to escape me, so I put my dagger to his throat. "You are my prisoner young warrior. If you please me I may let you live and treat you well, but if you do not obey me, then I will finish you now."

There was fire in his eyes, and I said, "I have been known to free those who please me well. You will be of no use to you comrades if you are dead."

He frowned and spat in the dust but stopped his struggling.

I lifted his filling weapon to see his balls and found that, as I had thought, he had a fine low-hanging set. I wrapped my hand about the skin high up and felt them, tugging and squeezing them as I examined them. They were, indeed, very full and heavy ones I knew I would like to suck on. Finally, I looped another cord through the one at his wrists, leaving it long so that I had something with which to lead him by.

I took the leather cord and pulled him up to his feet and then led him away. He walked slowly, restricted by the cord at his ankles. I pulled him on, and he fell several times before he got used to the restriction and learned how to trot quickly behind me in fast, short steps.

We soon joined my companions and, mounting our tired horses, left the site of our ambush with the booty we had collected loaded in our saddlebags. A short time later we came to a shady place by a small spring and stopped to refresh ourselves and rest. But once I had drunk my fill and allowed my prisoner to do so also, I led him away a short distance and found a shady patch of soft grass.

"Lie down," I told him, and he fell to the ground in exhaustion.

I had him lift his legs, and he obeyed me quietly. I ran the cord by which I had been leading him through the one that tied his ankles then tied it to the base of the tree we were beneath. He was now in a most useful position, his legs up and pulled back and open, and his arms also pulled back so he was hardly able to struggle. I pushed his thighs wider, and he gave me no resistance until I knelt between them and tore off his meager clothing. He began to curse me and struggle then, but however much he wanted to, he was unable to move out of my reach. I quickly took his weapon into my mouth and sucked it eagerly, while at the same time, tugging on and squeezing his sac and balls. He made pained struggling cries that I hardly noticed I was so much enjoying the feeling of his weapon growing and stiffening inside my mouth.

Soon I slid my sucking mouth off him and admired the way he had grown under my attentions. He was a very goodly size and thickness. I stroked him then and took my mouth to those balls of his, sucking each and glad of their length. My own weapon had become as hard and big as was usual when I was enjoying such fine amusement. And it would soon need to be wrapped inside my captive's' unexplored passage. I lifted his firm, full ass and looked for the first time on his rear entrance. It was small and tight. I dropped my mouth to tongue it and felt it clench and open and clench again as I attacked it. But I was throbbing now and did no more than spit on my fingers and probe briefly inside his tight asshole with them before I knew I had to make my way inside regardless of his readiness.

I wiped the liquid dribbling from my own slit about my huge weapon's head and placed it against his entrance. He began to cry out protests and to writhe about to escape me but was too restricted to move about much. I grunted and groaned as I forced my weapon into him, feeling his tightness about my cap as it passed the first part of his entrance. I was vaguely hearing the young warrior's cries but was too much occupied in forcing myself deeper into his painfully tight passage. I rested then, glad that he quickly opened to me, and I moved deeper. His hips bucked, and I took a tight grip on his balls to still him, as my own weapon continued to move in. I was pleased at his tightness. I finally had myself in to the hilt and cried out, "Yes. Victory."

I could hear his cries of pain and his grunts at my movement inside him, and I took his own now hard and big weapon and stroked it till the young warrior came. He spouted a goodly amount of seed in several strong bursts, and I heard his moaning change from pain to wonder at the feel of me inside him as he opened up to me and I began to plow him. I lifted his hips as I rose to my knees and began a deep, long exploration in and out of him. My hips made a good sound as they met his firm hairless ass, and I worked him hard for some time before I arched back and roared, as my seed exploded from me deep inside him. I stayed buried and stroked him back to stiffness, by which time I was also able to plow his now well-opened body for some considerable time.

The young warrior now moaned and writhed under me in pleasure, and I saw that his face now had a look of wild need on it. He opened his eyes and held mine as I fully left him and then drove myself back inside his passage and to the hilt. With each huge splitting thrust, he cried out, "Yes. Again, Yes, again." When I had released my seed into him again I withdrew.

"No, no, I want your weapon driving inside me," he cried.

"You have pleased me well, young warrior," I said as I released the cord from about the tree. He was watching me with hooded eyes as I reached for his nipples and rubbed each one. He gasped wide-eyed at the feeling this gave him, and I laughed at his innocence. "When we next rest, I shall see what other pleasures you have for me," I said.

"I want to feel your great weapon buried to the hilt in me," he begged, looking at me.

And I had every intention of giving him a great deal more of what he wanted.

The Barbarian and the Pirates

The merchant in Tyrins said that I would need some protection if I planned on taking my goods to the island of Cythera. There had been reports of pirates around the south and western islands, sea folk showing off their power at sea. Tantalos was an old friend, and though I was reluctant to incur any more costs for my journey, I knew he was reliable and that his advice had always been good in the past.

"I am handy with a sword myself," I reminded him, hoping he'd not press me to hire anyone. "I am also young and strong and always keep my merchandise near me," I added. "I have traveled this way before and have learned to look after myself."

"I tell you, Mydon, you would be wise to hire a guard. And there is one such here now I can highly recommend. He accompanied my son, Akamos, on his journey back from the north."

I shrugged, and sighed, "I trust your advice, Tantalos, old friend, so if you really want me to take on this man, then I'd look a fool to the Gods if I didn't. And I leave tomorrow on Iros's ship so—"

"So, I will have him here to met you, Mydon, and make the bargain, in the morning."

"Yes," I said, wearily thinking that my profit on this trip was looking very thin already and wondering if I might be better selling what I had in Tyrins and returning home. But no. What I brought back from Cythera would be where my profit lay, and if I needed to keep this man Tantalos recommended with me till I returned, then, so be it.

I made my way to the dock, and finding Iros's, boat I made sure our arrangements were still good and told him of my new companion. Then I returned to Tantalos's warehouse and spread my blankets on the floor near my merchandise and slept well that night. At dawn I wakened to find my friend calling my name and joined him in his warehouse and found my new companion already there.

I stared at him as he lounged on a bale of wool in front of Tantalos.

"He is a barbarian. From the north. How do you know I can trust him?" I whispered in my friend's ear.

Tantalos shrugged. "I have trusted Konan twice this summer, and he has not failed me. Now he wishes to travel to the west, and the stories coming out of the western part of the ocean tell me you may need someone to help protect your merchandise."

I had been staring helplessly at Konan all through this talk. He was a tall, solid young man, whose bronzed body rippled with muscles as he reclined there with his legs spread, and my eyes were drawn to the mound pressing up against his soft leather loincloth, the only clothing he wore. My knees were going weak, and I was feeling hot.

"Um. I will take him," I said, "I will take him. He seems to be very . . . um, strong."

"He is. In all ways," Tantalos said, looking at me knowingly. "But you will have to make arrangements with him."

"So, Konan, you are agreeable to protecting me and my cargo on the voyage to Cythera?" I asked him,

"I would not be here if I wasn't," he replied, and he immediately demanded a fee I was surprised at, as it was almost exactly what I was willing to pay. I offered him less.

"If you do not want me," he replied, shrugging his shoulders and rising off the wool bale to his full height, "Then I may as well go."

"No, no," I said. "But. . . ."

I wanted to haggle more. It was in my nature to do so, and I was always known for my ability to make a good bargain. But . . . "You have a bargain," I said, and he reached out his huge hand for me to shake. A strange way to seal a bargain, I thought.

After this, Tantalos's servants served us breakfast, Konan eating mightily and saying little, even when directly questioned. When we had eaten, I made my farewells, and asking Konan to take up my chest, we left the merchant's house.

Konan followed me to the boat, as a servant should, carrying my chest full of merchandise. It had rested securely at Tantalos's house overnight, but I was glad of Konan's strength now, as it was some distance to the dock.

"And what do you trade in?" he asked. "This is very weighty."

I was glad of an excuse to walk closer to him and to look at him. "Amulets," I said. "And images of the gods, worked in bronze."

"So, you are a smith," he stated.

"I can work metal," I informed him. "But I follow the life of a trader."

He said nothing more, and I had no excuse not to walk ahead of him as a master should and wished I was walking behind him instead. I wanted badly to watch him moving before me, see his thighs work and his butt roll, watch his back and shoulders and . . . yes, I already ached for the huge barbarian.

That evening on the boat, as we sailed past the islands near Tyrins, I said to him, quietly, so no one else heard. "You may sleep here," indicating the portion of the deck where my sleeping mat lay.

As a patron of the trip, I had a place set aside for me to unroll my mat and sleep in some privacy away from the crew, who were a smelly and rough lot.

He looked at me innocently and replied, "While you sleep, master, I will guard you and your goods. But when you are awake, I shall perhaps close my eyes for a few moments during the day, if you will guard what is yours and wake me if I am needed."

"Of course," I said, blushing foolishly.

Once the boat was moored for the night, I lay down dejectedly, unable to think of anything but the great barbarian's magnificent body and what lay beneath his loincloth. And pulling my manhood from under my tunic, I stroked it until my seed sprouted from its tiny mouth, not just once, but three times. I sighed then and was instantly asleep, but I confess I woke in the night and did the same again, as I looked across at Konan, my barbarian guardian, seated nearby and just visible in the pale moonlight.

For four days we traveled thus, my mind full of unsatisfied dreams of lying with the giant, and with no sign of any pirates. Often we sighted and hailed other boats that passed us, or that we passed, going in both directions, and word of murderous pirates to the west was on all lips. On the fifth day, we crossed a large tract of open sea that lay between Greece and the large island of Cythera. Our destination was near, and as there had been no trouble, I began to regret having the barbarian with me, as so far he had done nothing but cause me to have restless nights.

That evening, as we ate on the deck, the steersman, who was lookout then, cried out, "Ships, sea folk ships," and all hands dropped their food and ran to the railing to look out and to gather their oars. I ran with them and saw that two boats were approaching us from the west. And I knew the helmsman was right, as I had seen a sea folk boat before, when I had visited Rhodes.

I grabbed hold of Konan's arm. "Now is when you should earn your money, barbarian. And how do you plan to fight two boat loads of men?" I asked him angrily, as the crew set up the planks of their benches and sent their oars out through the ports and began to row to increase the speed of the ship and attempt to escape the pirates.

Konan seemed unconcerned but walked back to the hatch leading to the cargo area and climbed down. I followed him into the hull, having no idea what he intended and having no ideas of my own. The crew of Iros's boat was tough, but we had no chance against two ships bent on stealing our cargo, and we were unlikely to escape with our lives.

Konan grasped the handles of my chest and lifted it up and carried it to the hatchway, then pushed it up on deck.

"What are you doing? You cannot give them my chest," I said angrily. "What sort of guard are you?"

He smiled at me and moved to the rail; away from the approaching boats and out of sight of the rest of the crew, who were now on their makeshift benches, rowing as hard as they could but with their weapons ready at their feet.

Konan had a long rope and tied it cleverly about my chest and lowered it over the side of the boat. And when it was hidden below the surface of the sea, he walked along the boat to the steering oar and, bending over, tied the rope off among the others that held the oar to the boat. Even I, who knew what he had done, would not have known that my chest was lashed to the oar. I gaped open mouthed at his cunning.

"So, barbarian, you have my goods safe. Now what about us?" I asked, wondering what other clever tricks he knew. "Shall we hide under the water too?"

"The sharks might find us too tempting," he replied, and I laughed at the barbarian's poor knowledge of the sea, as there were no sharks in our sea.

"Come," he said, "I have more rope to use." He now guided me toward the mast. "Now stand against it," he told me, and I did, curious as to what he would do.

But in moments he had me tied to the mast with the rope he held, and I shouted, "Let me loose, you. . . ." But before I could finish, he had stuffed his loincloth into my mouth and silenced me.

All I could do then was whimper in fear, terrified the pirates might torch the ship, and me with it if he left me tied there. But I was also looking down to the barbarian's manhood, and my whimpering was as much for the size and thickness of what I saw there, rising up from between his thighs, as for the danger I was in from any approaching pirates.

I could do no more than grunt as he finished tying me to the mast, finally having me strung up with my arms raised and spread, and my wrists tied to the cross piece that the sail was attached too, and another rope wound firmly about my chest, binding me tightly to the mast.

Once he was done, he gripped my linen tunic by the hem and tore it from me so I stood there naked. And I looked down and saw my own manhood rising up to greet me, and if I could have, I would have gasped in ecstasy as Konan wrapped his huge hand about it and fisted it, as I writhed, and tried to breath.

"I will clear your mouth," he said. "If you convince me that you are enjoying this," he said, smiling at me broadly.

I nodded and opened my eyes wide and tried by all means available to let him know that I was willing to appear to be enjoying whatever he was going to do to me, if only he would remove that soft leather from my mouth so I could breath easily again.

He moved his hand to my sac and rolled my nuts about, and I rolled my eyes and moaned as best I could, not having to pretend at all. Then his fingers ran back behind my sac, and I parted my legs involuntarily as those long fingers found my rear entrance. I was looking down and panting as well as I could through my nose. The sight of his huge organ bouncing against my belly and hitting at the tip of my own cock had me hard and dripping. And the sight of his hand disappearing between my thighs as I felt his fingers run over my rim was even more arousing.

He reached his free hand to my face, and suddenly I could breath and I gasped for air as his mouth found mine, and his tongue entered it just as one of his fingers pushed up into my channel.

I moaned as I never could have with his loincloth in my mouth; then he was kneeling between my thighs and had lifted my legs up, having a hand behind each knee, holding them high up so that my ass was pulled up, my cheeks parted, and my hole exposed to him. I whimpered and rolled my head as his mouth found my puckered hole and his tongue took up playing with it.

As I rolled my head I saw the pirate ships hardly thirty ship lengths from us now, and our crew frantically pulling on the oars, to speed us away from them. Unfortunately, I was sure the pirates were gaining on us. Our crew sat on the benches with their javelins, knives, and swords at their feet, each man ready for battle, but I also noticed that several had their eyes dreamily fixed on me and the barbarian as he worked my ass with his tongue.

When he had soaked my entrance and softened me up, he pushed his tongue into my channel, and I moaned and writhed in pleasure at this. Then he lowered one of my legs, and that hand went to my entrance, and it was no longer his tongue I felt widening me, but his fingers. They were so long as to reach my spot easily and so thick as to be stretching my channel when he had only two of them pushed inside me, and I was bucking and crying out at the stretching I was getting. And I cried out louder as he worked three fingers into me.

I noticed vaguely that the crew were rowing in a frenzy as the pirates gained on us, their ships taking the wind better, and traveling faster across the sea between us, even without oars.

Konan fucked me with his fingers until I was loose and those three fingers had slid in and out and were able to twist and rub inside me and I had shot my seed over my chest and belly several times. Then, as the pirate ship came within hail of us, he rose up and lifted my other leg high again and, finding my gaping hole with the head of his huge sword of hard manflesh, he rammed it deep inside me.

I screamed. Screaming at the pain of his forceful entry and nearly fainting on that first rough thrust. Then he withdrew some inches, but immediately rammed his huge cock into me again, his pubic hair rubbing my ass as he bottomed to his limit in my ravaged passage. I screamed again and meant it, I was sure he was splitting me, and I screamed when he did it again. My cries were so loud I had no doubt that not only our crew, but the crew of the approaching ships could hear. And they could also see me and knew exactly what was happening. Konan bottomed again, but this time my scream turned into a moan before he had drawn back, and when he rammed home again, I howled in anticipation of the pain turning to pleasure, and with three more thrusts it was pleasure more than pain, and I cried out, "Yes, yes."

And as I rolled my head about in my abandonment to his fucking, I felt a boat jarring thud, and saw that the leading pirate boat had joined us. Her crew leapt across the rails with ropes, planning to tie them to us.

As the sea folk pirates boarded us and began to fight our crew, Konan continued to plow me deep, and shouted loudly, "If you want a treasure, I have it here."

And he leant back and withdrew his sword almost completely from my sheathing channel, so all could see his huge length and thickness, and then he drove back into me, to my loud cry.

"Ah, few men can take me as he is," he shouted then, showing them again almost the full length of what I was taking and burying it deep inside me again.

"I have made him ready, and if you spare the lives of our crew, you may have him for your own pleasure while you are on this boat, and you may take all the cargo we have if you leave us undamaged."

I could not believe what I was hearing, but I was unable to do more than cry out and moan at my complete possession, as Konan plowed me deeply and steadily.

Our crew drew back unexpectedly, dropping their weapons as the sea folk captain came over and pulled his own good sized tool out and began to stroke it to hardness as he watched Konan plowing me.

When he was satisfied with what he saw, the pirate captain threw his head back and laughed. "Your cargo and this man's magic ass are mine, with not a drop of my crew's blood shed. I am more than happy with this bargain. Now, finish your taking of him so I may have a turn."

Konan bowed his head to the pirate, and with a flurry of fast and hard strokes, he came deep inside me, throwing his head back and letting loose a mighty roar as his seed spouted out of him.

I felt his seed flooding me and sighed; then his tool pulled out with a huge noise, and his man-juice dribbled out of me as he lowered my legs. The pirate captain called over two of his men, instructed each to take hold of one of my legs and raise it up high and wide, and then he slid his own cock into my well-prepared channel easily and plowed me deeply until his seed also spouted inside me. Then the pirate next highest came and took his turn. I was swimming in their seed, and it was running out of me as the third one filled me.

Then I was untied and laid across the rail and taken that way from behind by several more pirates as I drifted into oblivion.

I awoke to find the ship quiet and gentle hands wiping my sore, bruised ass with some soothing oil, and I groaned at the pain and opened my eyes.

"Konan," I moaned.

"He is gone," a voice said.

"My chest, my merchandise," I gasped fearfully.

"In front of you," the voice replied, and I looked up, and there it was not feet away form me, and I sighed and asked, "And Konan, where is he?"

"Gone. When the pirates left, we discovered he was nowhere to be seen, but you're chest was on the deck, dripping water."

After that, I drifted off into a deep sleep. And I dreamt of Konan riding me again, his mighty weapon filling me as no other man's ever had.

Konan's Dream

I knew it was a dream. The spirit of sleep takes me to strange places sometimes, and this was most definitely one of the strangest of them. I knew, as one does in dreams, that this was some future place, which explained the fragile-looking building—not of stone, or wood and stone, but of some thin-cut timber perhaps. Very square and neatly made, but easily overwhelmed. No matter.

I had opened my dream eyes and found myself lying on a soft patch of grass beneath a tall, spreading tree in full leaf. It was warm, and I was happy to be dozing there in my dream and closed my eyes again. Hoping the dream took me to some more interesting place.

"Ecusxe em, mu, owh rea oyu?" a voice called out from not far away, and I opened my eyes and lifted myself up on an elbow to face the direction the sound came from.

A bare-chested man with a short beard and wearing some strange bright red-colored loincloth stood by the fragile-looking building, looking toward me.

He was not young, but not old either, lean and well formed, with his chest and legs showing firm muscle. In my dream I had woken with my weapon filling, and now it lurched as if wanting to conquer this stranger, and I squeezed myself lightly and saw the stranger's eyes follow my hand.

"Good day to you, stranger," I replied to him.

"Waht rea oyu doing in my garden?" the man asked. (Fortunately the magic of dreams finally allowed me to understand his speech.)

"This is my dream, friend," I replied, laughing. "And if this is your garden, and you do not like visitors—well you will have to take that up with the spirit of dreams," I added, getting up off the soft grass and moving to investigate him.

For this dream man had whatever it is a man must have to interest me, and my weapon was growing under my loincloth in recognition of this. And as I stood up, the dream man lowered his eyes to what I was now showing between my thighs before looking up and asking, "Who . . . what . . . ?"

He appeared to be confused, his urges warring within him. "I am Konan," I replied, "the great barbarian."

"Well, whoever you are, this is private property. So, you had better leave," he replied.

I reached him and, tucking a finger into the waistband of his loincloth, I pulled, drawing him closer to me and wrapping my other hand about his back and pulling him in even tighter.

He struggled against me. "I think you . . . you should go," he gasped, "or . . . or I will . . . will call the police," he stammered, but I could feel his own organ rising as it was pressed against my thigh.

And in my dream I wanted the release his body could provide me, and having no care for what friends of his might be called to join us or to fight me, whichever these police he wished to call were, I rubbed my engorging manhood against his. And he did not call out to those police.

"Ahh," I sighed, as he quivered and moaned to my touch as I stroked his chest and twisted the nipples hidden in the tangle of glossy hair on his chest, which continued down to beneath his soft, red loincloth. "You are a fine looking man," I said, "and of fine size also," I added, reaching my hand down and feeling how long and thick his own weapon now was as it pressed higher on my thigh.

"Not here. Not here," he gasped and waved an arm to the side, and I looked about and saw that the small, roofed enclosure near us had furniture inside it, and I released him and allowed the man to lead me toward it.

As he passed through the doorway into the small shelter, he stopped and turned to me. "You are a giant in every way, but you cannot be Konan," he said and hesitated there as if he now didn't want to enter the building with me.

I shrugged, not caring what he thought, for I know my name and what sort of man I am, and I just lifted him up and lay him over my shoulder and carried him into the pavilion, with him kicking and beating at my ass.

"Ahhh," I said, seeing in there items of furniture and knowing what would suit my purpose best. As I put him down by the back of a wide, low chair, I stripped off his red loincloth, which was not of the usual type, being closed at the sides. Then I turned him and lay him over the back of the chair, which was so wide it was perhaps a throne in this future place. But it moved away from me as I lay his weight across it, and then it swung back. I smiled at this for it suited my purpose admirably.

But the future man struggled now and twisted about to face me and muttered, "We need protection. A condom. I have some in the house."

"If we need protection, I have it here," I said drawing my sword from the scabbard that lay across my back. "This is the only protection I have ever needed, my sword and my wits."

The future mans eyes went wide, and his own manhood, which was already most interesting and well filled, stood higher, obviously impressed by my fine steel sword.

"From the land of the Great Mogul," I said, showing him the ivory inlaid grip, "and made of the finest steel."

"Yes. It's . . . um, very fine," he replied, impressed, "but you don't need it. Not here," he assured me, "I meant protection from diseases, a condom, a sheath a . . a French letter?"

I knew not what he talked about, as I had no sickness, and I ignored him, instead turning him back around and pushing him over the back of the chair. He moaned as I quickly plunged a finger into his ass. By the way he took it, I knew he was no stranger to such treatment. But the chair's swaying unsteadied him. So in spite of his struggling and cries of, "No. You can't do that, not here, no . . . No," I found some smooth cord, and tearing it from the items it was attached too, I bound his hands to the arms of the chair with one to each side, wide apart, and I bound his legs to the sides, spreading them very wide, which opened his ass to me in such a way that his cheeks were parted and his hole was visible in his crack.

Now my hands were free to run over his body and explore him, as he was now well restrained and held in place for me. His muscles were well defined, and I was unsure of his age, he was so firm, the gray in his hair gave him an air of wisdom, while his body spoke of passion and lust, and his own tool was a very goodly size and thickness for a mortal man, and his balls full and heavy. He was a most satisfactory companion to find in a dream.

Then, while I held his cheeks fully parted, my tongue dug briefly at his hole to wet it and open it and ease my entrance into him, and his rim twitched at my attentions. Hmmmmmmmmm. My fingers dug again into his channel, and I ran them about till I found that place he wanted to have rubbed most, and he moaned. "Yes, there. Oh. Yes. Oh. Fuck me."

I smiled in anticipation, knowing I would fuck him long and hard in many ways, and I moved my cock head to his hole, and he lurched and cried out. I reached under him and rolled his balls in my palm and found his engorged pole pressed hard to the back of the wide chair. I pulled it back to me and fisted it as I pressed my cap to his rim; then I released him and, instead, pulled his cheeks wide and pressed in, feeling his resistance and hearing his cries, a sudden loud cry from him signaling that my cock head had passed the ring of resistance trying to keep such a huge, thick weapon from conquering and possessing him completely.

I was almost oblivious to his cries now, inflamed as I was with lust and need and knowing only that he could take me, as I sunk myself slowly into his center.

He writhed against his bonds, and I stroked his manhood as it spouted his seed. Then he slumped forward and moaned, and I continued my journey to his heart. He opened readily for me then and took me manfully, finally groaning and moaning as I began to move inside him, sliding in and out and working his tight channel for my pleasure as he moved his hips about, giving me access and fine sensations.

I soon began to rock the moving chair back and forth and worked my hips in rhythm with its rocking, as did he, and we continued this for some time till he was hard again and I was ready to fill him with my seed. Then I slammed into him, deep and hard. And he cried out all over again at being torn apart as I flooded him with my first load.

Then I untied his legs and lifted them and drove straight into him again, his ass tighter now, and fucked him more before pulling out so I could untie his hands. Then I was entering him again and pulling his body up and his head back to mine so that we kissed, his mouth sweet and giving as I used my hands under his ass to support him and lift him up and down on my throbbing weapon till I came again. My cum was now running out of him and down onto my own thighs.

Without withdrawing from him, I moved about the chair and sat in it with him in my lap and rocked him on my manhood as it hardened again and then had him ride me, first leaning forward so I could see my great tool moving in and out of his tight hole and then facing me so that I could tongue his body and suck and nip his nipples and taste his pits as I stroked his throbbing tool to a third spouting.

He was a fine man and gave me great satisfaction, and I filled him yet again with my seed and left my weapon dormant in him as he collapsed against my chest, moaning softly and sighing happily as I lost my size within his passage.

I must have drifted off into the world of sleep then, as I sat there rocking gently on that wide chair with him lying against me. For the next thing I knew was awakening on the deck of the pirate boat, being rocked upon the Ionian sea.

Ahh, yes, it was a strange world I had visited, but a very fine man I had taken as my lover there.

The Fine Young Nobleman Meets the Barbarian

I was on my way to the court of the Great Mogul and had left my family's home only days before, when my adventures began. My father, a prince with little more than his ancient title, was sending me to court to further my education and hopefully to improve my station in life. Fortunately, I had grown into a very fine-looking young man of good health and education, and at nineteen years of age, I was looking forward to going to the court to make my way in the world.

No expense had been spared in setting me up so that I would arrive at my destination in a manner appropriate for a young nobleman of good family. I rode in a palanquin with six bearers, all of them good-looking men. My fathers' lands were not particularly large, but the men of our land were all well made and strong. We presented a fine sight as we passed along the road, with several mules following behind bearing my possessions.

I lay back in the cool shade of my curtained vehicle, thinking about my brilliant future while being gently rocked by the steady rhythm of my bearers' swaying strides.

It was the fourth day of my journey, and I knew that that night we would be at the last stop before my destination. I was daydreaming about the court and about the fine men and women there, and I admit, tugging at my cock idly in accompaniment to my pleasant thoughts. This happy activity was occupying me, when I became aware of a sudden jolt and a stagger among my bearers. I frowned at the intrusion. Then my palanquin stopped moving and I heard raised voices.

I stuck my head out between the silken curtains and looked about. But I immediately pulled my head back inside. What I had seen in that brief glance outside was not good. A great barbarian on horseback had a sword to my chief bearers' throat. I found my own sword buried among the cushions and grasped it, then pulled the curtains aside.

"What is the meaning of this delay?" I demanded in my most commanding voice.

There was a sudden silence, as everybody looked my way. The barbarian, with his huge rippling muscles glistening in the bright sun, lowered his sword from my bearers' throat and slid nimbly from his horse. He strode over to me, his muscles playing with the light as they moved beneath his golden skin. My cock lurched at the sight of him and was making a noticeable statement when he stopped in front of me. He looked me over, running his eyes from my head to my crotch, where my interest in him showed clearly in the way my fine silk pantaloons were tenting.

My sword arm seemed frozen by his presence, and I was dismayed at my helpless state. Then I gasped, open mouthed, as he laid a huge hand on my chest and pushed me back into my palanquin, where I fell among the cushions, with him joining me and my sword fell from my hand as I felt the palanquin dropping to the ground under the extra weight.

"I am Konan," my attacker announced, as he tore my fine silk pantaloons from my lower body. He eyed my hard, throbbing weapon, rubbed his huge thumb over its cap, and pressed it into my already-leaking slit. I groaned and trembled, automatically tilting my hips and spreading my legs wide to show him my asshole.

He laughed at me and leaned forward, covering my mouth with his, and I opened my lips to him, almost overwhelmed by the masculine scent of him. Then he wrapped a huge strong arm about me and lifted me up to him, as he tore my coat off and fastened the fingers of his other hand to a nipple. I bit his lip as he worked the hard lump of dark skin, sending shivers down through me to my already-aching manhood. I had my hands on him as we kissed, running them over his incredibly hard, full muscles. I found his nipples and squeezed them both and then lowered a hand to his loincloth, seeking his weapon. I shuddered when I felt a mammoth tree trunk there, hard and standing proud and tall. I moaned as I slid my hand up and down it, guessing at its length and trembling at the thought of it possessing me. Because I had no doubt this was what Konan intended his weapon to be used for.

Konan moved his mouth down from mine to my chest, biting my nipples in turn so that I cried out, then moving his big tongue over me, wetting me and arousing me more. His mouth finished on my cock, and he swallowed my eight inches as if they were nothing. I thrust my hips violently at his face as he sucked and tongued me. Then he dropped me back onto the cushions, and I lifted and spread my legs for him and he grabbed my butt and lifted it to his lowered head. I reached out wildly to steady myself as I gasped for air, my hands finding the uprights at the corners of the palanquin's frame. I grasped these and held myself steady for his mouth to work my ass. His strong tongue slobbered over my tight, but well-used entrance, pushing into it while his huge hands enveloped and spread my cheeks wide. I moaned as I gripped the palanquin's frame and bore down on his hard probing tongue, helping it enter me, making me moan loudly.

Konan moved his mouth briefly to my balls, and I moaned even more for him.

"You are a very fine young nobleman," he said, as he moved his mouth back to my hole.

He lowered my butt then and turned to straddle my face, and I gaped at the huge tool he was lowering to my mouth. I could take only a small part of it in comfortably and not more than three quarters of it even with great difficulty. As I sucked and caressed that huge weapon inside my mouth, he leaned forward and pulled my thighs back under his arms to give himself perfect access to my anus, I was choking on his huge rod and bucking my hips as he poked his thick fingers inside me and worked me open with them, sending me wild as he stroked me in there. Finding the spot that set my cock dribbling copiously.

I wanted him to quickly go on to the obvious conclusion and moaned, "Yes, yes," loudly when he removed his huge weapon from my aching mouth and turned himself to kneel behind my butt. I looked down as he wiped his huge rod over my inner thighs and over my own manhood before positioning it at my wet, slightly gaping entrance. I knew I wanted his cock fucking into me, and I reached down and held the tip of it just behind the nob, keen to help him guide it in.

Konan threw his head back and laughed loudly. "So, my fine young nobleman is eager to be taken by a huge barbarian, is he?" Konan asked.

"Yes," I replied panting in anticipation, "Yes, fuck me Konan. Yes. Yes. Yes," I gasped wildly, pushing my ass down while pulling his huge poised cock to me.

Konan pulled my hips down to him. He pulled me onto that great rod, and I cried out at the pain of its entrance, and then again, and gasped as he pushed in over my most sensitive spot, slowly working into me deeper and deeper. I cried out repeatedly as he continued to drive himself in, overcome by his size and wondering if he was going to tear me apart. But that huge weapon continued its relentless journey of discovery inside me. Going where nothing human had been before.

Many men had been in there before Konan, but never so far in, nor fit so tightly. He chewed at my neck as he worked himself in deeper. I writhed in pain again, gripping the frame of my palanquin as I tried to open my ass wider for him. After a while the pain of him entering me had lessened and I was feeling incredibly overfilled instead. My own hard cock was throbbing and dripping as I moaned and breathed raggedly. He moved himself deep inside me, and I cried out briefly again. Then he moved again, and I moaned at the pain and the incredible feeling of being massively stuffed and stretched by him.

He massaged my gut by fucking me, so I opened up for him, and soon I felt waves of pleasure run through me from his cock sliding slowly in and out of me. Then he was pounding my ass, and I was crying out in wild abandoned ecstasy. He added his cries to mine before he roared like a great animal and arched back, driving himself hard into me, and I cried out at the feel of his cum flooding me.

I came up my own belly in huge spurts and jerks until I was spent and lay back almost senseless. Konan collapsed across me but left his massive tool buried as I wrapped my thighs about him, wanting to keep him deep inside me, now that I had accommodated him.

Konan soon hardened inside me and pulled my legs free and moved out till only his cock head was still inside me, and he worked that in and out over my spot so that I moaned and writhed in pleasure, desperate to push myself back down on him.

Then Konan stopped. "No don't stop," I cried, before I became aware of a commotion outside and my palanquin's curtains were parted. I turned to the intrusion as my ass was emptied and Konan grasped his sword and made to attack the intruder.

Konan's size behind his sword's sweep pushed the intruder aside and Konan leaped from my palanquin. I lay there stunned and panting, my legs spread wide and raised up, showing my abandoned cum-slicked gaping asshole, and my hard and throbbing cock. Before I could recover myself, the intruder had returned and climbed in below me. I moaned as he dropped his armored skirt, and I saw a more than adequate cock standing rigidly to attention for me. In a moment that weapon filled the barbarian's place, not so fully, but well enough, and I was again holding the frame of my palanquin, grunting loudly and working my ass to the intruder as he plowed me deeply.

When he had come, he sucked my balls and then worked on my own throbbing organ, taking its measure. "A fine piece of equipment you have here," he said. "And whose fine cock do I have the pleasure to be sucking?" he added, holding my cock to his mouth and forcing his tongue tip into my slit.

I was crying out and moaning so I was hardly able to answer him with my father's name.

"Ahh," he said, between sucks on my now purple cock head, "So, you are the young nobleman coming to court to make his fortune?" he mused.

He paused for a moment, again taking the measure of my now rock-hard cock, which I doubted had ever been larger or thicker. "Well, I am the Grand General of the Great Mogul's armies," the intruder said, "And now that I have tried these fine assets of yours, I assure you that you will be a great success at court. In fact, I myself need a new adjutant to serve me and hope you will accept the post."

And with that, he finally let me come, my juice spouting across my palanquin in thick streams. Then he began to plow me again, and I grasped the frame of my palanquin as I moaned loudly and sighed happily at my good fortune in rising so high so quickly and the wonderful fucking I was having.

The Barbarian Tells How He Escapes Capture

My weapon had remained sheathed inside the fine young nobleman while we kissed. He lay back among the cushions of his curtained palanquin, while my muscular barbarian body covered him and my hands roamed all over the full rounded muscles of his chest and his flat, hard belly. I was well on the way to being recharged and about ready to begin plowing him deeply again when I was distracted by a commotion outside.

The young nobleman moaned and moved himself on my buried weapon, his passage caressing me to greater size and hardness even as I struggled to regain my senses. Then the curtains of the palanquin were suddenly parted, and I beheld a finely dressed intruder wearing glittering armor, but of sudden and greatest concern to me was the long curved sword he carried at the ready.

My cock disengaged with a sucking sound as I grasped my own sword, lying among the cushions. I threw myself at the armored intruder leaning through the curtained opening, but my mind wasn't on it. That was still stuck back with the feel of my recharging cock buried inside the passage of the muscular, golden-skinned young nobleman I was leaving behind me.

The young nobleman's cries of, "No. Don't stop. Don't stop," followed me even as the intruder met my slashing sword with his, and my arm shook from the impact. Unfortunately, this man was no fancily dressed amateur, and I was still regathering my strength as well as my wits.

60

We joined in a fierce battle of brutal swordplay that took us from the shelter of the palanquin's curtains, and then I saw that, unfortunately, the finely dressed intruder was not alone. But I was. My two barbarian companions were nowhere to be seen, but my opponent had a dozen uniformed soldiers encircling us with their curved flashing swords at the ready.

The intruder was a skilled swordsman. I, being a tall, broad, muscular barbarian, relied greatly on my strength, so when several of the bodyguards joined on my opponents side, I was hard pressed to save myself from being killed. I had no wish to be cut to pieces, and the matter of whether I might escape was settled when my sword went spinning from my hand as the result of a badly placed strike that saw me unbalance and crash to the ground.

I was briefly stunned, shaking my head as I recovered and looking up to find half a dozen steel blades pointed at my throat and chest. I lay back in apparently helpless submission, with my mind turning to a later clever escape rather than trying for an unlikely one now.

My opponent, the armored intruder, came up to stand over me and ordered that his men tie my hands. "I am the Mogul's Grand General," he said to me, "And you, barbarian, have caused me much trouble and have now dared to attack a nobleman on the road to the Great Mogul's palace."

The general continued looking down at me for some moments, seeming to eye the weapon I had lately sheathed so pleasurable inside the fine young nobleman's channel.

Then the Grand General turned to a slightly built soldier beside him. "Come, what do you think of this barbarian's great tool?" he asked, and the man stepped up and reached down and stroked my weapon, then cupped and squeezed my balls as if measuring them too.

"Very fine," he said admiringly, having tested my equipment.

"As long as he is safely tied, you may do as you wish with him till I return," the general said, and turning he went over to the palanquin and entered it. I saw the curtains close behind him and had no doubt what he intended to do in there.

Two soldiers were kneeling by me then, one on either side, one taking my balls in his hand, the other my cock in his mouth. I was soon growing for them and grew even more at the sound of the young nobleman's cries of pleasure coming from the palanquin.

Then a man raised my legs and made to finger my hole. I stopped being quiet when I felt him and struggled and kicked. But my captors had me well tied, and those not enjoying me had their swords ready still. So, now they tied ropes about my ankles and pulled me up and dragged me hobbling to the palanquin, from which the general was just emerging.

I was spread-eagled at sword point and tied fast at ankles and wrists against the frame of the palanquin, inside which I had so recently enjoyed plowing the handsome, well-endowed young nobleman. And in spite of my anger, my cock hardened more at the memory of his tight, willing passage enclosing me. He was a fine young nobleman indeed, as the Grand General now standing before me had confirmed for himself, I was sure, by taking him and fucking him after I had been forced to withdraw.

Now I was at the general's mercy, and I raged and tore at my restraints, throwing myself about and violently rocking the well-made palanquin. I heard the young nobleman inside cry out in fear, and my unsatisfied lust for him increased my rage.

"Stop," shouted the general. "If you destroy the palanquin, I will finish you with my own sword."

I looked at him and bared my teeth and roared, but I stopped my violent shaking. It had achieved nothing so far, and there were a dozen men of his about me with their swords drawn. Silently, I cursed my two companions for abandoning me so.

"Cowards," I thought, angrily spitting in the dust to show my disgust at their abandonment of me.

The general moved in and worked my cock himself now, running his hands along it, over its veins and ridges, and teasing the slit in my huge head, almost getting the tip of his little finger in to it.

"Lets see how big this weapon of yours is, barbarian," he said, stroking me to make me grow. His hands were not unwelcome, but he was, until I saw something that made me encourage his attentions.

"Come, why don't you feel that inside your ass?" I said to him, "Or is it too big for you?" I cried out rudely, taking the attention of all the men there, many of whom were laughing at me now.

"If anyone's ass is to be filled, it will be yours, barbarian," the general replied, encouraging his soldiers' laughter, as he showed me his own respectably sized cock, which he pulled hard and throbbing from his fine robes.

Then the general tore down the curtain at my back and stepped in close behind me, though I struggled and roared abuse. I was Konan, the great barbarian, and no man touched my ass. But I couldn't stop the general from parting my cheeks, and though I struggled and raged, I soon felt his mouth exploring me. I tried to resist the feeling of his tongue at my hole. I tried to deny the pleasure I was feeling from it as he circled and teased my rim. I raged more, but soon I was wet enough that he could begin to explore me deeper with his fingers, while one of his soldiers fell to work on sucking my rod.

The soldier had a fine, firm sucking mouth and squeezed my balls in a most pleasurable way. I was caught between the mouth at my engorged weapon and the fingers seeking inside my passage, and suddenly I groaned, unable to resist the pleasure the general and his man were giving me.

And now I also finally saw what I had been hoping to see, what I had only had a glimpse of earlier. So that though I had resisted before, now I willingly moaned encouragingly for my molesters. The Grand General opened me up with his fingers, working them firmly in me, so that I cried out at the unwanted invasion, feeling a stretching and opening I had never felt before. He seemed to fill me so much I wondered if I might be feeling his whole fist inside me. But then he withdrew his fingers to replace them with his cock. I cried out in agony as he worked that large weapon of his into me. I knew that it was a fine, large piece of equipment and feared my tight, unused ass would have trouble taking it.

I roared in pain as the general groaned with pleasure and moved in deeper, but he was soon pulling out again, before making me moan and whimper as he moved back in. I cried out and then groaned, as my passage resisted his efforts to go deeper. But as he worked himself in and out of me, I must have opened, as my moans became ones of pleasure, and it felt surprisingly fine. He moved back in, and I felt a great sensation of pleasure such as I had never felt before and realized that he was as fine a swordsman with this weapon as he was with his fine steel sword. I moaned at the feel of his cock going deeper and cried out as he began to plow me with long strokes.

The soldier at my own cock had me in a tight muscular sucking embrace inside his mouth, and I soon roared as I filled his throat with my hot, angry cum. The general plowed me deeply and furiously took advantage of my orgasm, and I moaned with pleasure, tightening my ass on him in my ecstasy. He flooded me with his hot cum, and I took it with surprise. Then he withdrew, and I sagged on my bonds and moaned.

The soldiers standing about laughed, but their amusement was cut off by a piercing scream, and then another, as my two companions returned on horseback, raining savage lethal blows on my captors. The general grabbed up his sword and swung about with it, raising and meeting Uran with a great clanging strike that almost tore the steel from the hands of both of them. But Uran was on horseback, and the general had no chance, and a second jarring blow had his sword falling to the ground as he grasped his wrist in agony.

The general's soldiers were all soon dead, or dying, or had managed to escape, and Siri rode up and cut my bonds with four clean slashes. I pulled free and smote the general to the ground with one sweep of my great right arm. He lay there in agony as I recovered my sword and pointed it at his throat and his eyes glittered with hate as he looked up at me.

"You will be hunted to the farthest corner of the Great Mogul's domain," he cried in a rage.

I shrugged and then bent to tie his hands together, ignoring his cries as I used his damaged wrist roughly.

My companions, Siri and Uran, finished off the injured soldiers and suddenly the road was quiet. Quickly Siri took the leading rein of the loaded mules and left with them. And I went to the damaged palanquin and found the fine young nobleman lying there almost as I'd left him, naked among his cushions. I could have had him again immediately, but I knew that it was time for us to leave.

"Come," I said to him, taking his hand and pulling him up, seeing his cock already half engorged at the sight of me. "You are coming with me," I said gently.

"But I have to go to the Great Mogul's court," he replied haltingly, looking confused. And he was even more confused when he stood outside his curtained vehicle and could see the dead soldiers and the bound general lying there on the dusty roadway.

"But all my possessions?" he cried, looking about for the vanished mules, "My palanquin, my bearers?"

"Gone, or ruined," I said bluntly.

Uran had the general standing and was helping him onto a spare horse, and I whistled for my own horse, which came trotting up to me. I jumped up into the plain saddle and pulled the fine young nobleman up before me, resting his naked butt against my naked manhood, my loincloth ruined, where it felt very fine.

When Uran had gathered what booty there was to take from the dead, we left, riding toward the nearby hills and our hidden barbarian camp.

Kidnapped by the Barbarian

The Mogul's general had plowed me almost as deeply as Konan the barbarian had. And before he left, he assured me that now he had enjoyed my "asset's," he knew I would be a great success at the Mogul's' court.

When the general was gone, I lay back happily among my cushions with my legs wide, feeling better fucked than I had ever been before, and thinking about my brilliant future. But I also longed to feel the great barbarian Konan's huge weapon plowing me deeply again.

Suddenly, my palanquin shook violently, and I cried out in fear, before lying back exhausted, hearing mumbled voices and groans from outside. But in a short time the curtain opposite me, at the other end of my palanquin, was torn down and I saw the back of my great barbarian tied, spread-eagled against the sturdy frame of my vehicle. His large, full, rippling muscles and great size aroused me even in my tiredness. In a moment the Grand General came behind Konan and knelt to part his muscular cheeks and began to tongue his entrance. The palanquin shook as Konan struggled to escape that tongue, but he was well tied. And the Grand General, I knew, was a fine hand with a weapon, be it tongue or cock, and soon he was fingering Konan's ass with firm, experienced probing and the great barbarian was crying out at a pain I knew he would soon find turned to pleasure.

I began to stroke my own cock as I watched them. And I was right, as soon Konan was moaning and his cries were the ones of a man wanting more. The general entered him with his fine large weapon, and Konan cried out painfully again at the size of it. But it was not long before the general was plowing my great barbarian deep, and Konan was moaning with pleasure. It was a sound I found aroused me more, so that my cock grew to exceptional length and hardness at the sight of them fucking and the sounds they made. The general came inside Konan, and I was almost ready to come myself, when a sudden bloodcurdling scream was followed by another, and I froze in fear, expecting to be killed at any moment.

Two mounted bandits came into view, slashing wildly down at the Grand General and his soldiers, felling the soldiers left and right, before one rode up and freed Konan with a few quick slashes of his sword. I fell back upon my cushions both from my relief to have my great barbarian rescued and at my shock at the massacre happening just beyond the silken walls of my palanquin.

I stayed low, among my cushions, afraid of what may happen to my barbarian Konan, but afraid also of what might have befallen the Great Mogul's general, who had also fucked me well and had assured me of a fine future at court.

Konan returned to my side soon after and looked down at me, and I was pleased to see the desire in his eyes and his cock growing even as he looked at me.

"Its time to leave," he said, and taking my hand, he pulled me up and led me outside, where I had a rude shock.

The Grand General lay in the dust of the road, bound at wrists and ankles, with half a dozen of his men lying about him bloody and dead, and I felt ill to see my mules gone and my palanquin damaged. I was at Konan's mercy, and though I wanted his great weapon sheathed deeply in me, I was suddenly lost and worried about my future.

* * * *

I had the naked young nobleman up before me on my horse, his fine ass resting against my naked manhood, as we departed from the scene of the massacre and headed into the surrounding hills. In little more than a mile, I had hardened again, and my cock wanted to be buried inside the fine passage of the young nobleman resting against me. I reined in my horse under a lone shady tree, then set my hand between the young nobleman's shoulder blades and pushed him forward, over my horse's' neck.

"What are you doing?" he asked, turning his face to look at me.

"Do you want to ride this fine weapon of mine again?" I asked, holding my cock and stroking it.

"Yes. I have not told you, Konan, as you left me so suddenly, but I have never had such a great, wonderful, weapon inside me before, and almost more than anything I want to have it fill me again," he replied, which pleased me and was as I expected.

His hole was visible between his fine, full ass cheeks, and he moaned loudly as I tested it with my fingers to see how loose and wet it felt.

"You will take me easily," I told him with pleasure, finding him still well stretched and lubricated. So, I did no more than push him further forward and hold my cock head to his entrance then pull him back onto me. My young nobleman cried out and tried to open himself for me as I lowered him, and my weapon drove up into him. After his earlier use, he accommodated me more quickly, though he still cried out and groaned loudly as the hair about my manhood reached his entrance. Now I held him there with an arm about his waist as I urged my horse into a gentle canter.

"Oh no, I can't take it like this," my young nobleman cried out, arching his back as the motion of my horse moved my throbbing tool about deep inside his passage.

The motion of my cantering steed worked my cock extremely pleasurably inside him and he was soon moaning and gasping, pulling up his knees to open himself wider as he rode me, held firmly in place by my strong encircling arm. The feel of his channel embracing me and the loud frequent sounds he made were a very pleasant accompaniment to my ride.

I came three times inside him before we arrived at my camp, each time filling him with my hot cum and making him moan with great pleasure, though he moaned a great deal in between as well.

Uran and Siri had arrived before us, and I reined my horse in near where they were seated about a small fire. The Mogul's Grand General was still bound and now tied to a nearby tree, and the young nobleman's pack mules were tethered to several others, their loads removed and stowed safely inside a tent. Seeing all was well, I pushed my young nobleman forward again until I could free my cock, and it made a pleasant sucking sound as it left his hole, leaving his ass slightly gaping from its long stretching on our ride. I slid from my horse and helped the groaning young nobleman down, having to support him, because his legs were too weak to hold him up immediately.

"You have ridden me so hard I cannot stand," he said, falling against me and moving his mouth to mine, so that I took him in a deep kiss and stroked his cock until he came again up my hard flat belly. I knew he had come before on our ride, and I was pleased at his obvious virility.

I then set him aside. "Go to the river to refresh yourself," I said to him, turning him to face the fresh, clear stream that ran through the valley beneath the shady trees where we had made our barbarian camp. "I will join you there soon and we'll see how well you like taking my weapon in the water," I said, pushing him toward the steam and watching him stagger as he walked toward it.

I spoke briefly to my companions, Uran and Siri, and then went to the Grand General and knelt and inspected his bonds.

"You will pay for this, barbarian," he said through bared teeth.

"I think not," I said. "I think it shall be you who pays, my fine general," I told him, having some good idea of how he should be made to pay for his treatment of me and for his release.

Then I stood and went to the river, where I saw my young nobleman lying on his back in the shallow water. I approached him and said, "Stay floating as you are."

I took his feet and pulled him out into deeper water until I could kneel on the sandy bottom with only my head above water. Then I spread my young nobleman's legs wide and pulled him toward my mouth before pushing his belly down lightly. This set his cock at a level so I could feed it into my mouth, and I sucked strongly on it as I played with his balls. Then, when he was moaning and hard, I released his belly letting his hips rise slightly in the water before resting his thighs on my shoulders and moving my mouth to his hole. I found it slightly open still and slipped my tongue inside it, to his sudden moans and splashing, as he quivered from the feel of it entering deep into him. Finding him so ready, I stood slowly, letting his legs loose so that they opened wide and fell to my sides, and once standing, I ran my hands under his hips and held him up. Then I had to do little more than slide my engorged weapon into his eager open asshole as I moved to stroke his body and cock and work his nipples.

He began another long session of moaning and crying out as I plowed him deeper than I had before, and for far longer. Eventually I roared and came, filling him again with cum; then I helped him by wrapping my hand about his own manhood, so we both shared the pleasure of jerking him vigorously off.

The Fine Young Nobleman's Story Continues

When I finally arrived at the Great Mogul's court. I had proudly and gladly entered the household of the Mogul's Grand General as his adjutant and his personal favorite. I now lived in the general's wing of the Mogul's great sprawling marble palace, with its glittering white domes and cool colonnades, its tiled courtyards, enclosed gardens, and splashing fountains.

It was a fine and luxurious life, and I had also been put into training immediately for a high position under the Grand General in the Mogul's vast army. And I had trained hard and was fast becoming more muscular and athletic than I had been before I arrived, working hard to prove myself worthy of the high position the general had made available for me. Because in spite of being the Grand General's current favorite, I knew I would not keep my high military position for long unless I proved to be a satisfactory commander.

I now saw myself making my fortune through the plunder I could take and the rewards handed out to those who led the Great Mogul's victorious armies into battle against his enemies.

When I was not sweating and proving myself to the Grand General upon the training grounds that lay in the valley behind the great palace, I proved myself to him upon his couch inside the palace. And in every way I lived a life of great comfort, physical exertion, and much pleasure.

Now at the end of a hard day's training, I stood on the fine, brightly colored mosaic floor of the marble bathing hall with its finely worked pictures of plants and animals, and a lean but muscular bath attendant poured scented water over me to rinse off the sweat and dust of the training ground. And while I was bathed, I thought further about my situation. Having helped the Mogul's Grand General to escape humiliation at the hand's of the mighty barbarian Konan, I had assured myself of gaining my present high place in the Great Mogul's court.

But I sometimes wondered if I had made the right decision.

Yes, I was sure there had been nothing but a rough and dangerous life ahead of me if I had stayed with Konan and his barbarian companions. But I had never been taken so well as the great muscular Konan had taken me, nor felt such pleasure as his massive weapon had given me. Nor had I ever trembled and writhed, or cried out and moaned as he had made me when his great weapon was driving in and out of me.

Not that the Grand General did not satisfy me. He was a finely made man of large appetites and with a goodly sized weapon, which he took great pleasure in exercising inside me. And he had introduced me quickly to the other pleasures he enjoyed, and I had thanked the gods for the virility that let me enjoy them frequently.

He enjoyed particularly working his weapon inside my passage while I worked mine in some other fine young soldier's channel. And often he ran his fingers into me beside his pumping weapon to gain extra pleasure, and I still cried out with passion when he did this. I had arrived at court already well used and was now so open from good use that I was able to take any man in the Mogul's court with ease.

Many young men of the Grand General's company were also well equipped and showed their considerable experience in the way they handled their weapons when working them inside me. But I felt a hopeless longing for one man's weapon still. I longed for the great barbarian Konan's great meaty sword, plowing me deeply. None could match the great length and thickness, as well as the stamina of that muscular giant of a barbarian who had first taken me in my palanquin on my journey to the Mogul's palace.

My thoughts had stiffened my own weapon and the muscular bath attendant, knowing my desires well, had dropped to his knees behind me, separating my cheeks so he could get his mouth to my well-used entrance. He tongued me eagerly, and I leaned forward against a nearby marble column and sighed and made happy little noises as his tongue speared inside me. Then I moaned and wriggled my ass back to him as his tongue shared my loosening opening with his long fingers.

A passing young commander of good physique observed that my own long, hardening tool was unattended and stepped in beside me and ran his fingers about it in a way I had never felt before, as he brought his mouth to mine for a kiss. I was well engaged now, and all thoughts of the barbarian Konan had fled. After some dueling of tongues, I pushed the young commander to his knees as the man behind me finally fed his weapon into me. Once he was buried to the hilt, I rocked my hips in time with his pumping of me and made good use of the young commander's face, quickly filling his throat with my juice.

I then saw that the young commander's own weapon was erect and throbbing as he knelt beside me on the brightly patterned mosaic floor of the hall. I pulled him up and sucked him into my mouth and showed my pleasure at his hardness by taking his creamy juice and swallowing it gladly as my own tunnel was being given a final thrusting filling by the attendant behind me.

But once the attendant had withdrawn his weapon from my passage, I could only think of Konan's huge size, and knew I needed more than the attendant had to offer me to be truly satisfied.

I left the bathing hall and walked naked through the cool corridors of the palace to my fine apartments, where I collapsed on the down-filled silk pillows of my canopied bed. I sighed, knowing that the Grand General himself would soon arrive, having had to speak to his commanders before he bathed and relaxed with me. He was not Konan, but he always worked his weapon well inside me, and I lay there stroking myself in readiness, but dreaming of Konan as I waited.

Suddenly, there were noises and shouts in the passage beyond the fine gauze curtains at the archway that led into my apartment, and I lifted myself up to pay attention. I thought I heard a familiar voice, and my heart leapt and my cock throbbed, but I knew I only imagined it. For I believed he was dead.

The noises got closer, though, until suddenly there was Konan, yes Konan, alive, being led into my chamber in chains. He was struggling with the guards leading him, but then he stopped, as if frozen, when he spied me lying naked among my silken cushions.

Konan fixed his eyes on me, raking my body from foot to head with his glance, and his eyes burned with anger but also with something else. I had believed it when I had been told that he was dead and was overcome by the sight of him.

"So, my fine young nobleman, again I find you lying indolently among your cushions. But this time I am a prisoner dragged into your presence, not a bandit waylaying you," he said with arrogance. "So, why have you had me brought here?"

"I was told you were dead," I said foolishly, as he quite obviously wasn't, but I was not able to think clearly and answer him sensibly.

Konan's body was gleaming from the sheen of sweat filming it, and I saw his great muscles were as full and round as ever. He was breathing heavily from his exertions, and this was making his chest swell and fall, the golden muscles shimmering with each breath.

I rose up on my bed, kneeling with my tool in my hand still hardening and lengthening, my thighs spread wide, and my ass pushed back in anticipation. I was immediately filled with lust and unable to lift my eyes from Konan's huge, partly engorged weapon. It hung between his great muscled thighs like a club, and I desperately wanted it to beat its way inside me. I moaned at the memory of how well it had filled and pounded me a few months before.

"Well I am not dead," he replied, stepping forward, "and I ask you again, why does the fine young nobleman who betrayed me to the Mogul's Grand General have me dragged before him naked?"

"I did not ask to see you," I replied, confused, knowing how I had ached to see him though I had been told he'd been killed after I had aided the Grand General's escape from the barbarian's riverside camp.

The guards, I suddenly realized, were linking Konan's chains about the nearest of the slender delicately carved marble columns that circled my chamber supporting the domed ceiling.

"Ahhh," Konan sighed, now eyeing me all over in such a way that not only was my weapon hardening, but my breathing also was becoming uneven and my rim twitched.

Konan moved his arms, testing his loose chains and moving toward me as he did so. The guards stood back smiling, and I was afraid of what Konan might do to me for having betrayed him. But I was unable to move away and remained kneeling among my cushions. The great barbarian stopped at the foot of my bed before reaching out his arms to grip my thighs and topple me over backwards among the soft down pillows. Then he was gripping my ankles in his great hands and pulling me toward him.

The barbarian had lost none of his strength, and moving his hands to my hips, lifted them easily. I trembled, knowing that even as well used as I now was, I couldn't take his great weapon inside my slick passage without some preparation. But lifting my hips higher, he slid my ass off the bed and up his belly, closer to his face, and I widened my thighs, and my legs flopped back so my feet rested against his shoulders.

Then Konan's mouth was on my entrance, and I pawed at my cushions and silken sheets and cried out in small cries as he roughly wet me down and opened me. I kicked my legs about and he stopped and, grabbing an ankle, twisted one of his chains about it, holding it wide; then he caught my other ankle in the same way. I hung now from the chains coming from the columns, my ass level with his great pecs, my arms still pawing at the bed to steady me as I hung, swaying, from the chains.

Then his tongue was rimming me, and his great fingers were entering and probing me as I moaned and tried to steady myself against the bed. But his fingers plowed me, shaking me about, and he rocked me back and forth on the chains as he rotated and spread his four fingers in my passage. I was soon moaning with pleasure, hardly aware of the pain of the chains digging into me. Then he flipped the chains off my ankles, dropping me on the bed and, with a great grunt, came down over me, biting at my nipples and then my neck as he pressed the head of his huge tool at my entrance.

"Yes, Konan. Yes!" I gasped, even as I pulled my thighs wide and wrapped my legs about his hips and steeled myself for the pain of his entry.

I screamed as he pushed his cap past my rim and entered me. I wanted him still, but I was certainly not well prepared. He stopped and bent to kiss my mouth and grasped my weapon, my hands trembling as I used them to tease his own big hard nipples. Then he moved in deeper, and I wailed and twisted about, trying to widen myself for him. Finally, he had taken possession of me, and I groaned and cried out as he began to move inside me. He used my hips like handles, gripping them in his great hands so he could twist and rock me, while his huge weapon moved about inside my channel as it never had before, reaching and testing hidden parts of me, straining me so I thought I might be torn apart. I yelled and moaned with pleasure to have him stretch and stroke me so, quickly coming in fountains of cream across my belly and my fine silk pillows and still he worked himself inside me.

"So, you moan for this giant as you never moaned for me," I heard the Grand General's voice say angrily as a final pulse of juice spilt from my weapon.

"Oh, no," I cried, "No, I moan as well for you," I gasped. Then the general's tool was in my gaping mouth, and I struggled to suck it as he took my head between his hands and pulled me back and forth.

For a moment I had wondered at the general's words but was immediately lost in my sucking and opening my throat for the Grand General's own large tool. Both men worked me hard, my body rocking back and forth, and soon I knew they were each trying to outlast the other.

My jaw was beginning to cramp up and my entrance throbbed as my gut spasmed when I heard the pounding in my ears as Konan pressed his thumb into the slit in my cock head, seeming to release my pent-up juices again in a sudden flood, while the general spurted his seed down my throat. Once the general withdrew from my mouth, I cried out and moaned as Konan continued to plow me deeply.

"It seems only this barbarian can truly satisfy you," the general said angrily. And I could do no more than paw at my silken pillows and roll my head in mindless ecstasy in response.

"Did you think otherwise?" Konan replied in a deep, rumbling voice, his hands stroking my body as I rocked with his pounding rhythm.

"I do not want a man who cannot be satisfied by me," the general said. "If only this great barbarian can satisfy you young prince, then you may join him in the dungeons."

I caught the general's words and wanted to plead with him that he was man enough for me, though my arching, writhing body and loud helpless moans of pleasure made it clear I would be lying. Konan finally chose that moment to fill me with his own hot seed, and I was unable to get the words out anyway, because his weapon throbbed inside me. I moaned loudly as I felt his juices flood deep inside me, and my entrance closed on his huge weapon and held it as it pumped another spurting of his hot seed into me.

"Take them away," the general ordered.

Konan pulled out of me with a soggy slurp, and able to move at last, I turned my head. "No. No," I cried after the

Grand General's departing back, seeing my fine life and great and prosperous future fading fast. "No. No!" I screamed in an agony of despair.

Konan bent and gripped my chin and kissed me deeply, then winked at me, and I wondered if he had gone mad, or was glad I would be joining him in the palace dungeons. Which was also madness from my point of view. But then he stood and flexed the great muscles of his chest and arms before suddenly jerking his fists together. Nothing discernible happened. Then he jerked his arms together again, pulling on his chains, strain showing in his face, and I heard a great crack.

I rose up among my silken pillows, still recovering my senses as his juice ran out of my hole and down my thighs, and I saw the stone columns Konan had been chained too broken in several places and beginning to fall apart. I gaped in awe at this proof of his huge strength. Then I saw the guards were looking up at the marble dome of the ceiling, which seemed to crack and shudder as I stared up at it with them. A sudden great cracking noise sent the guards fleeing into the passageway, yelling in panic.

Konan grabbed my arm and pulled me up, "Time we left here, my fine young nobleman," he said, smiling, and I jumped to the floor and stayed close by him as he heaved his chains free, wrapping the loose lengths about his shoulders as we ran for the walled garden beyond my apartments.

Konan climbed the garden wall easily and pulled me up behind him. But at the sound of a great crash, I turned to look back, only to see the dome of my fine apartments reduced to a cloud of white dust, which quickly spread out and engulfed us.

"Now to get rid of these chains," Konan cried, as we dropped from the wall, and he ran like the wind along the deserted pathway behind the wall, pulling me along behind him in the direction of the stables.

Imprisoned

If the fine young nobleman was before me today, I confess I would still have the desire to take him long and hard. He was a very fine young nobleman, who had whatever it is a man needs to have to make me want him enough to be foolish about it. And each time I had him he caused me a great deal of difficulty.

That first day I took him in his palanquin and then back to our camp, where I fucked him long and hard until I was spent and thought I had taken him to exhaustion also. But, no. He had awoken in the night and crept off to inspect the goods that had been his and that my companions had carried off. They now sat in a tent in the camp we had been living in for the previous half moon while we raided wealthy merchants and others traveling poorly guarded on the roads to the Great Mogul's palace.

It was a time when no poor man's lands were safe from the grasping hands of those above him. And Siri and Uran were both disposed farmers who had taken their complaints to court and found themselves laughed at and kicked out and warned not to return, so that now they had no other way to live and to keep their families fed than by stealing.

When the young nobleman went to examine those goods, which had been his but were now ours, he was caught by Siri, who was roughly honest with him about the future of what had once been his possessions. The fine young nobleman was sent away to sleep by the fire without any restraints and was in a rage, for he was always most concerned with his fine possessions.

In the morning I awoke and found him gone, along with our horses and the Grand General who had been left tied to the tree. It was too late to shout at Siri for his foolishness, and the signs showed that they had escaped some hours before. So, we took the smallest and most valuable of the loot we had collected and, tying it up in bundles that we slung across our backs, we abandoned the rest. We had no choice, and we set off at a trot toward the hills, where we could most easily get lost and evade armed and mounted pursuers.

But fortune was not with us, and we had not gone far when we heard the noise of pounding hoofs approaching . At least six horses. So, we broke into a run, knowing our chances were slim of making the rocky hill trail before the horses overran us. The bundles of treasure were holding us back, but the families in hiding would not survive without them, and Siri and Uran would not let theirs go.

I understood their situation, and knowing that I should not have brought the fine young nobleman to our camp and let him roam free, I threw them the bundle I carried and turned back, as they ran on.

I quickly scaled a spreading tree that overhung the trail and drew my sword and waited.

The first rider lost his head to my swinging blade and the next was knocked off his horse. The third was ready for me, and I had to dodge his blow but was able to fall on the fourth and use my knife to silence him before I slipped to the ground and drew my sword again and stood in the path of the last two riders.

"The general wants us to take him alive," one of the armored warriors cried out, and I stood there, my body loose, my breathing deep and steady, readying myself for whatever came next. Meanwhile, the two warriors on their horses circled me, and the third recovered from his fall and caught a horse and remounted, so there were three of them, not knowing that all I was buying was time for my companions to reach safety.

Uran and Siri escaped, I know. But I was cornered and after tiring me, one of the circling warriors threw a net of weighted rope over me, and I was trapped like a wild animal. My sword was useless and torn from my hand, and my body was trussed up and bound, so that I could be slung on a pole between two horses and taken to the palace of the Great Mogul.

I had doubted I had long to live. But I regretted nothing. Since I became a man, I had lived wild and free, and it had been a good life. I had no regrets. I have none now.

I saw little until I was dumped into a cell deep in the palace dungeons. Then I struggled free of the net that had held me bound. And I waited. There was a small window in the door of my cell, and it opened often and faces looked in and voices muttered, but no one spoke to me, so I ignored them. Food—rough, tasteless food—was brought to me, and I ate it ravenously, I confess.

And then I slept. Another day passed during which I was fed and looked at, and again I slept. Then the next day the small window in the door had been opened, and a face looked in, and there was muttering outside, but the window wasn't closed and then, the lock on the door was turned, making a rough creaking sound. And the door opened a fraction. I stood waiting for I knew not what.

"I am coming in," a voice called out. "Know, though, that there are guards here with crossbows ready, and if you make any move to harm me, you shall be killed immediately. Do you understand me?"

"Yes," I said, and I did not doubt what he said. And I pondered if I might be wise to rush to my death now instead of rotting away in that hole, or worse, being taken from it and broken.

As I thought these thoughts, a young man slipped in to the opening and hesitated.

He was strong and muscular and dark haired. His body was naked above a pair of silken pantaloons and showed that he was no idle courtier, as not only was it a well-muscled body, but several scars lay across his shoulders as well. I knew him for a fighting man, and I always have some respect for fighting men.

He slowly entered the cell, and the door closed behind him with a heavy clang.

"The young nobleman the Grand General has brought back as his favorite has been foolish enough to tell me that there is no weapon to match yours, barbarian, even among the most favored in court. And I have come to see if he is lying," my visitor said.

He was very arrogant and proud.

"I show no man my manhood unless I am showing it to him as his possessor," I replied.

"Ho. Do you? Well, that suits me well enough if it truly is as the young nobleman says it is." He looked me in the eye now.

I laughed at my good fortune. "Then come here to me," I said, reaching out my arms to him.

He hesitated, and I saw a moment's fear, which I did not think less of him for. Then he stepped toward me, and I stepped toward him, and in a moment had my arms about his waist and had pulled him in hard to me. And then I reached a hand down to his ass and moved my mouth to his.

He tried to keep his mouth closed to me, but if I can, I will have my tongue in a man, and taste him and possess his mouth before I possess him in any other way. Finally, as I squeezed his ass, his lips parted, and I entered his sweet mouth and delved inside it as he gulped and reached for me.

I rubbed my engorging manhood against his belly and felt his own weapon grow, the fine silk of his pantaloons slippery and cool against my thighs.

He felt me growing, and his hand reached for my pole and tore aside my loincloth. He gasped at what he found, and I released his lips. My own hands tore off his fine pantaloons to reveal a black, glossy nest of thick hair and a fine upstanding sword throbbing above tight balls ready for spouting. My hand folded about him, and he groaned.

But I was in need of release myself after the last few days of danger and loneliness, and I quickly turned him and sank down to part his cheeks and tongue his hole so I could enter him.

He opened quickly, obviously well used, and my tongue was soon darting into him, making him spout his seed for me for the first time. I hurried then to lay a hand on his belly to keep him steady as I buried my fingers inside his channel. First one, then two, and then three.

"Oh, so big," he shouted. "If you are going to split me, I want your weapon buried in me, not your fingers," he cried to me, his body shaking

I obliged him.

The first entry was not so easy, but he quickly loosened.

"Yes, he was right. He was right." he cried out, as I moved in. "Oh, the gods, you are a giant. A giant. Oh."

He was widening himself and bent over and resting his hands on the cell wall and driving back to meet me even as I had difficulty entering him deeper. He yelped and cried out loudly so that the whole cell seemed to echo with his straining, and faces appeared at the window in the door and looked in and disappeared, to be replaced by yet other faces, and the mutterings and noises outside added to his cries and my own groans as I entered him and possessed him fully. I quickly filled him with a flood of hot seed, roaring loudly as it left me, that had him moaning for more.

Ahhhh, he had a sweet ass. And for an arrogant man he became most obliging as he lay beneath me.

"Ahhhh," he panted as I withdrew from him. "Ahhh," he sighed turning to look at my weapon which I knew would hardly wither before I entered him again, as I needed to take him more than once to be satisfied.

"Ahhh, yes, it truly is the biggest weapon in the palace," he sighed, kneeling before me and taking me into his mouth as far as he could, embracing me tightly with his lips, and stoking me with his tongue and throat.

"Ahhh," I sighed, "You are a fine young warrior," I purred to him as I gripped his hair and moved his head about.

Then when I was ready, I had him stand against the wall and move out only enough to give me entrance, and I entered him like that. Him tight and writhing as I enjoyed him to the limit.

When I was done, he slid to the floor, and his head lolled on his shoulders, and he looked at me in a daze.

"If I were staying here in the palace, I would hardly leave this cell," he said and laughed weakly. "But, fortunately, I am only passing through, or I would get addicted to you."

"But," he said, as he stood up slowly, "I will see that you are more comfortable here, as I have another day before I leave and would prefer to be ridden on a soft bed than on a cold stone wall," he said.

"If you wish me comfortable, good food would be more to my liking," I replied.

He laughed. "So, food and a bed. We want you strong," he assured me, then he turned to the door, "Open up, men. The show is over, and I am ready to leave."

A veritable feast was brought some time later, and a soft and large bed that half filled my cell. And that night the young warrior returned, and I rode him many ways and for most of the night on what was proven to be a very fine bed for fucking.

After that my life was an odd one, for though I was a prisoner, I was fed well and given many comforts and even allowed into the sun each day to work my muscles. And all this I gained by doing no more than fucking well the young men who came to visit me in my cell.

It was not the life for me, but it was a good life, and one where I lived to gain my freedom one day.

Unfortunately, after some months I met the fine young nobleman again.

One day I was surprised to have the guards enter my cell, and with one holding a lance to my belly and another a crossbow to my chest, I had no choice but to let them chain me. "We have orders to take you to the palace," the chief jailer said to me politely. "Orders from the Grand General himself."

"Why? Is this when I am punished?" I asked, suddenly concerned about my future, wondering if I had been complacent for too long and missed my chance to die nobly.

He shrugged as he bolted an anklet on me, "I think we go to the apartments of his favorite—whom I think you know," he added nervously.

"Ha," I said angrily, "The one who betrayed me and brought me to this cell."

The young nobleman himself has described most of what happened at that meeting. Again, I could not resist him, seduced by the way he opened his thighs and exposed his hole for me and the need and longing in his eyes. Ahhhh. Yes. He showed me such longing, such passion to be possessed. And then when the general had been, I knew I must manage an escape for both of us.

And as his apartments collapsed, he came unhesitatingly with me, over the wall and into the alleyway that led to the stables. But of course an escape was not to be. A troop of palace guards awaited us there, and I was trapped yet again and outnumbered, and the fine young nobleman fell to his knees crying, "I had no choice but to go with him. He is so big and strong."

Ahhh. I hoped I wouldn't see him again. He caused so much trouble for me.

I was returned to the cells, nervous for my future. Again I wondered if I should take my life, but that night a man who had visited me before visited me again and tried to reassure me that things would settle down. That the Grand General was only trying to test the young nobleman. And another came, and two days drifted by, and then three, and it seemed life might return to normal. I was still a prisoner, but I had little to complain of. I was alive, and one day I'd be free, as free as any man can be, once more.

But foolishly I begged the jailers for news of the fine young nobleman, fearful for what had happened to him. But again my misfortune had been to his benefit, as when he was dragged before the Great Mogul to be given his punishment and stripped of his titles, the Great Mogul himself took a liking to him, and he quickly satisfied that one's needs as well as he had ever satisfied any man's.

And then one day the chief jailer came again, and I was told the Grand General would speak with me and I was not chained when I was taken to him.

Barbarian Deliverer 1

"Rescue my son, and you can have your freedom," the Mogul's Grand General had said to me.

And now I clung to the top of the ruined wall that surrounded the rough cobbled yard in which the wiry Mongolian horsemen were holding him. The general's son was one of many the general had, but Kasim had been made a prince because he was the most handsome and most intelligent of all of the Grand General's sons. And all knew he was a favorite of the Great Mogul himself , as well as of his father, the Mogul's Grand General.

I had been shown a picture of Kasim. One painted by a great artist, to enable me to identify the prince when I found him, because I had been a prisoner in the Mogul's dungeons and had never seen the young prince who I was supposed to rescue, in the flesh. His golden skin and glossy black hair were perfect, and short glossy curls also cascaded across his chest, circling his dark nipples and descending in an arousing trail down his belly, to disappear below the waist of his baggy pants. I had felt my cock engorging at the image of him, and the general had pulled aside my tented loincloth to see my famous tool. I was well known in certain parts of the Mogul's palace for my manhood being as thick as that of a fine stallion, if not as long.

My imprisonment had not been very onerous, as I'd had a number of grateful visitors come to my cell and leave satisfied. But the Grand General had not been among them and it had been a long time since he had seen my manhood. Now he grasped my weapon in his short-fingered hands, and his eyes widened as the feel of his hands about me made me fill out further and harden to almost my full potential.

His head fell to my pole, and I gripped his turban as he moved his mouth over my big bulbous cock head. I grunted as his two hands strained to encircle me and his tongue played all about the small part of my length that he had inside his mouth. He pulled away before I shot my juice and called over a fine, tall warrior who had visited me privately and who now came over, trembling, and smiling at me.

"I am curious to see if a man other than the fine young nobleman can truly take such a massive weapon with pleasure," the Grand General said, "and as I know this young warrior claims to have visited you to have you bury your great sword inside him, I wish to see if he can take it now."

The warrior stripped of his rich uniform as ordered and lay forward over the back of a fine carved chair, inlaid with ivory and many colored woods. He gripped the arms with his hands and turned his head to look over his shoulder at me with fear and longing, as I moved between this spread thighs. I used spit and my thick fingers to prepare him as the watching general pulled out his own good-sized organ and began to stroke it.

The young warrior opened quickly to me, as I knew he would from our previous meetings, and I quickly had him moaning and arching his back and opening his legs wider, begging me to plunge my huge sword into him. I stroked his tool briefly, and he spouted across the floor in big spurts. And I heard the general moan as he became more excited at seeing this.

In spite of my fingering of his entrance and his passage, I had to hold my weapon steady to drive its domed head into the nobleman's loosened hole. He cried out loudly and writhed and opened himself wider as my cap passed the barrier at his entrance. Then he gulped and whimpered as I forced my rod in deeper, relishing the tightness with which his channel embraced me.

The general came, watching intently as I bottomed inside the young man to the combined sound of the nobleman's loud cries of pain and desire and the general's crying out of his amazement that anyone could take me so fully, as the warrior was doing. My fucking of the yelping young man was brief, as I had not had a visitor for two days, and I filled him happily with a goodly load of my seed. I was roaring as I came, accompanied by his high-pitched cries of ecstasy as he felt his insides being truly flooded.

I shortly after departed the palace on a fast horse, relaxed and able to concentrate on my task, and when I reached the small summer palace from which the young prince had been taken, I could begin to gain hourly on his kidnappers. But when I reached the hills, I abandoned my horse and continued on foot, running easily across the rough ground for many miles until I caught up with the raiders at an old abandoned fort atop a rugged hill at the edge of the desert. The entrance was sealed with old rotting gates that offered little protection but that hid much of what was inside from me, so that in the dark of early morning I climbed up the still-strong but weathered stone wall of the fort to get a view of what lay inside.

What greeted my sharp eyes was a small courtyard roughly cobbled and now home to a Mongol raiding party. And I saw through a fallen archway another roofless space in which they had their small, hardy desert horses stabled. And on the far side of the courtyard from me I saw their captive.

I moved in silence around the top of the wall until I was no more than fifteen feet above the captive but, unfortunately, some distance to one side of him, because the wall had an old section of roof jutting from it that would have hidden the captive from my sight had I moved closer. And there was little doubt that the travel-stained and dusty young man tied up below me was the one I sought.

His wrists were tied by a leather cord, his arms pulled up above his head, and the cord secured to a beam in the section of roof that remained above him. His rich clothes were dirty and torn in places, his jeweled belt gone, his silken turban gone, and his dark hair dusty and hanging to his shoulders. His many silk shirts hung about him in layers as did his fine silken baggy pants. His feet were bare, stripped of their jeweled slippers and just touching the ground.

But as yet there was nothing I could safely do to rescue him. I was alone and the six Mongol horsemen were standing about with their bows and arrows quivered on their backs, their short swords in the bets at their waists, and their knives handy in the narrow belts that ran across their chests. I would have to wait for nightfall for a chance to rescue the general's son.

I lay hidden and patient in a hollow in the top of the yard thick wall. Watching and waiting through the heat of the day. After a time the one I took to be the leader of the Mongols by his fine furred boots and richly embroidered vest stepped up to the young prince and spoke to him, and I listened intently to catch his words.

"I, Tiro, will have your aching arms lowered so that you can write that letter to your father, and they will stay lowered from then on, and you will be free to walk about the camp," the Mongol leader Tiro said.

"I will never write a letter begging my father to ransom me," hissed the young prince in reply, and he spat at Tiro, the Mongol leader.

The young prince was brave, but foolish. I was frustrated because I did not want him harmed before I could rescue him, but there was no way I could reveal my presence to him now.

Tiro wiped his hand across his dark face and then gave the prince the back of that same hand, and I heard the slap as it met his face and turned it aside. I doubted the young prince had ever known real danger before and hoped he did nothing else that was foolish.

But the Mongol lord was no fool either. He did not want his prize damaged seriously.

"I will have you write again to your father, this time telling him that you are alive still. But that you won't be if he doesn't send the gold I have asked him for," Tiro said as he removed his fancy leather vest, his quiver with his bow and arrows, his sword and his thick belts.

That done, Tiro stepped back up to the prince. "We will see if I can make you beg me to allow you to write to your father," he said, and smiled an evil smile.

The young prince looked at him with defiance. "Never," he said loudly.

Then the Mongol took hold of the prince's golden outer coat and ripped it from him, the prince exclaiming in anger. Then Tiro took hold of the next layer of fine silk shirt and ripped that open too. Then he did the same to the next layer and again and again, until Prince Kasim's sweating chest was exposed between the layers of torn fabric hanging at his sides.

The Mongol leader then moved his hands to the young prince's chest and stroked it and worried the dark hair rimmed nipples with his fingers, pinching and flicking at them, till the young prince jerked and cried, "I will never write to my father for you." But Tiro merely continued rolling both nipples between his fingers and smiled evilly at Kasim.

Then his captor walked behind Kasim and did much the same again, tearing open the back of each shirt until the prince stood with the rags of his finery hanging from his shoulders and fluttering like streamers in the breeze.

"I will never beg you," the young prince cried out through clenched teeth, as Tiro ran his hands over Kasim's back and nipped and tongued his neck and shoulders.

The Mongol, Tiro, laughed at Kasim's brave but foolish words and tore the silken strips from Kasim's golden body, the prince's body jerking as the fabric was ripped from his shoulders. And between tearing the brightly colored silken strips away, Tiro worried the young prince's nipples and stroked his hands over his body in an intimate way. In a short time, the prince stood there naked from the waist up. His muscular torso glistening with sweat and his chest heaving rhythmically as he breathed.

"Never," he said proudly, averting his eyes from Tiro's face.

The Mongol bent his head and sucked loudly on the prince's large dark nipples as the prince writhed and yelped, "Never, never."

Then his captor took hold of the waist of prince Kasim's baggy pants and tore the outer ones open so they fell down about his ankles. Then he tore the waist of his under ones, and they too fell about his ankles. And Tiro laughed a deep laugh of pleasure. As now the young prince stood there all but naked, his golden skinned muscular torso running down into his tight narrow hips, and the black glossy curls of his chest running down his belly, past his navel, to the lush jungle surrounding his long engorged cock and large balls.

I was most impressed by what I now saw of the young prince. What had been hidden in the painting of him I had been shown was as good as what had been on display. Yes, he was a very fine young man. And I saw with some interest that his cock was almost fully engorged. I reached under my loincloth and stroked my own growing tool. But I also worried at where the Mongol's treatment of the young prince might be heading.

"I will not help you to get your ransom from my father," the naked captive cried out bravely. "I will never write a letter to him for you."

Tiro laughed and stepped up to the young prince and took hold of his manhood and began running both hands up and down it and fingering and stroking his thumb over the cap.

The prince struggle and kicked, and two other raiders were waved in to hold his feet still, which they did. But I also noticed that they parted his legs as they held them. And the Mongol leader's hands had not left young Prince Kasim's goodly sized pole.

Then one of Tiro's hands went under Kasim's balls and back between the prince's legs. And I also saw the hand of one of the men holding his feet down go up to the prince's firm round ass and disappear, and knew that both were now fingering the young prince's hole as he writhed to escape them.

But their fingers had barely entered him when Kasim cried out and shot his load all over his captor. And I shot mine, my roar choking in my throat. Whatever result the Mongol leader had expected, it was obvious the young prince was at least partly enjoying what was being done to him.

The Mongol leader then pulled his own erect and throbbing tool free of his pants and stroked it over Kasim's belly and thighs, before moving behind the prince and stroking it over his cheeks. Then I saw him place his stubby rod to the prince's ass and stroke it up and down between his cheeks and over his entrance. Then Tiro knelt behind the prince, parting his firm round cheeks and sending his tongue between them, down to Kasim's puckered gate to pleasure. A gate I myself was now eager to open and enter. It was not long till Tiro stood again and placed a hand on Kasim's belly to hold him back as he began to feed his weapon in. The prince pulled on his restraints and rotated his hips and gave small 'cries that sounded more like ones of pleasure than pain, as the Mongol leader's short but thick tool progressed inside him.

Once his captor was in and had begun to pump him, the young prince moved his hips back and forth in eagerness, joining the bandit's plowing and making the fucking he was getting even deeper and more pleasurable for both of them.

It was not long before another member of the band came forward and swallowed Kasim's refilling tool and began to suck and slurp on it as he cupped the prince's balls and stoked his inner thighs. The young prince was moaning and begging, but he was begging loudly for thicker and deeper, not to write a letter to his father.

I saw the Mongol leader jerk as he shot his juice deep into the young prince's passage. And I heard Kasim cry out at the feel of it filling him and jerk in turn as he filled the mouth of the Mongol raider who was giving his weapon attention.

Tiro pulled out and whispered to the prince and stroked his hands over his belly and chest and sucked on his nipples.

Finally, I heard the young prince moaning, "Yes, yes."

The Mongol laughed and waved an arm, and one of his party came hurrying over bearing a flat board carrying a piece of parchment and pen and ink. The young prince's arms were released from their bonds, and once they had eased and he could use his hands, he wrote shakily but quickly.

The Mongol leader seemed very pleased that the young prince had done as he was asked at last.

Then Prince Kasim was tied up again. But the cord attaching him to the sturdy beam overhead was lengthened, allowing him to move about a little and sit down. But now prince Kasim was shouting at the Mongol leader that he had been lied to and was cursing the bandit leader Tiro in ways that I, a simple barbarian, had never heard before.

The bandit leader threw his head back and laughed loudly, then said, "Foolish prince, we have no man here as well hung as Konan the barbarian. He is a giant, and his weapon's size is legendary throughout the desert. And even if you could take him, he lies in the great Mogul's cells, captured some months ago by your own father."

With that the Mongols moved away and took little notice of Kasim, except to laugh at his antics as he kicked about, and tugged, and tried to chew through his bonds.

Barbarian Deliverer 2

As he fucked me, the Mongol's leader had told me that one of his raiders had a weapon as large as the famous barbarian Konan's, and the man would fuck me as well as the barbarian could. But first I had to agree to write the letter to my father begging for a large ransom to be paid for my release.

And, yes, in the throes of mindless lust and fullness and longing for that giant, I had heard such stories of I agreed and wrote the cursed letter.

The letter done, the Mongol bandits' leader laughed at the idea any of his tribesmen could be hung like the great barbarian Konan, and I was left in the dust humiliated, as one of the Mongol tribesmen mounted his small, tough horse, tied the lead of a spare beast to his saddle, and rode off toward the Great Mogul's palace.

Once the tribesman had ridden off with the letter I had so foolishly written, the rest of the raiding party relaxed about a small cooking fire and played a game among themselves, while drinking frequently from a skin full of some potent brew.

I felt shamed and humiliated, truly humiliated. And worse, I would have killed myself just then had I had the means available to me. For years I had tried to suppress my desire for other men. My old teacher, whom I had so admired, had made it clear that desires such as mine were unworthy of a noble prince. I had longed not to become like my father's favorites. They were all fine men in body, and good fighters, true, but to lie beneath another man, moaning and begging for him to fill them, was not worthy of a fine prince. If I had been like my father—who rode men fiercely, but never took them in himself—well, that would have been most acceptable to me.

Finally, in desperation, I had retreated to the small palace from which I had been kidnapped. I had gone there to pray and study and immerse myself in good teachings. To be celibate and overcome my urges.

In the Great Mogul's palace, there were far too many temptations, and the many beautiful wives I had in my harem were never able to quench my other desires. Ah. So I had retreated. Though my lustful dreams had followed me even there. As had tales.

Yes. I have to confess that I had dreamt of being taken by Konan the great barbarian, of feeling his immense sword of steel hard manflesh entering me and possessing my body. Always in my dreams he gave me a pleasure and aroused in me a passion I could not control.

Oh. I was so humiliated. And I wondered how the rough Mongol leader had known my secret desire and weakness. As he drove his thick tool into my inexperienced, but, no, certainly not virgin ass, he had said the name Konan, and I had quivered and spouted my seed. It was enough. Just that name. Oh, I was so wretched. And then he said he had one in his party as well hung as the great Konan, and that this man would take me if I wrote the small letter to my father. That was all I had to do, write one small letter, and the Mongol tribesman with a sword and balls such as the great Konan had would be mine. My flesh was weak. I moaned my answer, "Yes. Yes," and wrote out the letter in a daze of lust. Ah.

Now I was tied at wrist and ankle and attached to the stout timbers above me, as I lay naked in the dust among the shreds of my fine clothes. Meanwhile, my kidnappers were getting drunk on some rough wine they had. And soon, I thought, oh soon they will come and include me in their games. And, oh. I wish it were otherwise, but as I lie there, even my own manhood betrays me as I think this. It is telling me that it hears my thoughts, oh, in the moonlit courtyard, I feel my organ move and grow. My hand longs to reach for it and stroke it to it's throbbing release.

Stop. Stop. Unfaithful weapon of mine, I beg. And I think of the humiliation I have brought to myself, by moaning for Konan, by begging my father to ransom me. My father, who is a great man and a fine general, and yes, my noble father. Oh. How I wish I could end my miserable life.

Then. Well then there was a sudden confusion in the open courtyard where I was tied up. I saw a blur, a blur of muscle and flesh. Or I confess, I thought perhaps a demon had entered the courtyard. Suddenly, it was there beside me, hot and smelling of man and heat. Whatever it was, it cut my bonds and dragged me to my feet, but to add humiliation on humiliation, I was frozen with fear. Yes, I a noble prince, from a line of great warriors, stood there unbound and free, making no attempt to escape. And I stood with my mouth gaping open as the massive man creature disappeared into the shadow of the fort's high stonewall. But I traced his movement along it until he disappeared into the smaller area where the raider's horses were tethered and feeding.

In a few moments there was a flash and the crackle of flame, and the small but solid horses ran in a panic into the courtyard. The raiders staggered to their feet and tried to make some sense of what was happening, and some were trampled beneath the hooves of the panicked beasts. The beasts turned in every direction and finally I moved, finding my senses and running also, seeing the horses running toward me now. One of the horses still ran toward me, and the man on it's back reached down and swept me up and into his lap as he passed. Leaving only dust where I had been.

Then the giant turned the small horse about and we raced toward the entrance gate, and I shouted, "No," in fear, as I saw the rickety timbers barring our escape from the courtyard. But some of the wild, terrified horses that were loose were already running to it before us, as they could see the moon and freedom through the spaces in it. So that in a few moments, the timbers were nothing but splintered firewood, and we followed the escaping beasts safely through and onto the stony track that led down the mountain and back to the road into the valleys below. And beyond that, to home.

But I was held into the chest of a madman, or perhaps a demon. I stayed held there, on that wild ride down from the old fort until my rescuer, or the demon, pulled off the track into a pile of large boulders and slipped to the ground.

I had wild thoughts of kicking the horse on and escaping my rescuer, but he held the horse's reigns tightly, and I knew the beast was already tired from the fright it had had and from then carrying the two of us down the mountain.

Then the demon spoke, "We must change horses here, my fine young Kasim," he said in a deep rumbling voice, his breath rapid and his scent stronger than ever.

"Who are you?" I asked, suddenly finding my tongue, "Who are you that you know my name. Are you another kidnapper?"

Having felt the heat of him and his skin against me and seen his form close up now, I knew for certain he was no demon.

He laughed a deep laugh and threw me a piece of cloth, which I realized was to hide my nakedness, which I had forgotten about in our wild rush down the mountain.

"No. Quite the opposite. I want no more than to quickly return you to your father who has sent me to rescue you," he said, as he removed the saddle from our exhausted horse and placed it on one of the fresh horses he had waiting, hidden there among the huge rocks. The other was already saddled, and I wondered how they had got there.

The saddling done he turned to me and handed me a thin package. "Your letter," he said, and I took it and realized it was the letter I had written to my father and seen the tribesman leave with. "Your father says that if I return his favorite son to him, I gain my freedom. And a barbarian such as me values that more highly than anything else."

I was amazed. By many things. There was much to confuse me about my father in what he said. And about who this stranger was that my father would trust him so.

"Barbarian, you know my name. And as you have saved me, and my father, the great general, trusts you so. May I know yours?"

"I am Konan. The one they call Konan, the great barbarian."

When I heard this, I was stunned and horrified.

"No. You cannot be. No," I cried in disbelief. "No. Because of thoughts of you I have humiliated myself and written a letter begging my father to pay my ransom. Because of my dreams of you. . . .," in my confusion I knew not what to say. "If it was not for the longings and urges I wish I could cast off, I would not have been in the small palace where they kidnapped me so easily. If not for my humiliating desires, I would not have run from the Great Mogul's palace, or be here for you to rescue. And you, you would serve the just sentence given you for whatever crime you have committed." That last made me think what wrongs my desires had caused.

The barbarian laughed loudly as he mounted his horse and held the reigns of the other beast, waiting for me to mount it. "If you had allowed yourself to enjoy your natural urges instead of fighting them, you would be in the Great Mogul's palace enjoying yourself and taking your rightful place at your father's right hand. He has many great men about him who have cried out for his seed to spill inside them. As some of them have also cried to me, one even as he watched. Do not blame me, or those desires nature gave you for your misfortunes."

"You laugh," I replied angrily, "But no prince should long to be taken and possessed by another man. The honor . . ."

"I am just a simple barbarian," Konan interrupted me by saying, "I understand only good and evil, pleasure and pain, honesty and lies. I try to do good when I have a choice, I take my pleasure where I find it, and I only lie to my enemies. And that has kept me a happy man for all my life."

I mounted the horse he held for me, and we rode off, but I was disturbed by his simple view of things. Because I knew that he was right to say that it was my own fears and confusion that had led to me being the captive of the Mongol bandits. And I realized belatedly that when selecting his generals, my father did not overlook those men who took his manhood inside them. So that as we rode down the mountain to join the main road, I pondered what Konan had said.

We rode on into the dawn, till I was near falling from my horse with exhaustion and Konan seemed to be dozing as he rode. But he was instantly awake when we reached a small river we had to cross. And instead of crossing, he took a path along the bank, going upstream until he came to a clump of tall shady trees with soft grass beneath them, where we stopped.

"It is time to rest." He said slipping from his horse, "So we stay here till evening. And then we will ride on in the cool of the night."

When the horses were watered and hobbled, Konan spread two rugs out on the soft ground. Then he drank from a water skin, and while he drank, water ran down his body glistening in the golden hair that adorned his muscular chest and belly. But none reached his loincloth, and what lay behind it remained a mystery to me still. Then he passed the water to me, and I drank thirstily, water spilling and running down my chest also, but going on and wetting my loincloth, so that my organ's size and excited state was clearly revealed to anyone who looked at me.

I had been watching the great barbarian's muscular form for some time now, and it was as perfect as a man's body could be. Bronze skinned, golden haired, muscular, and agile. And I had some idea that the stories of how hard and long his manhood was were true. I was in turmoil inside, my own manhood telling me that my seed was in desperate need of release. My hole, yes my own asshole, quivering at the closeness of him.

Then Konan stepped behind me and wrapped his arms about my belly and lifted me up and carried me to the rugs and lay me on my stomach.

"What . . What are you . . . ," I stammered, my tool pressed against the ground beneath me and my thoughts confused.

His huge thighs straddled my hips, and he sat back on my thighs, pinning me beneath him. Then his big hands parted my ass cheeks, and I moaned. Moaned, knowing that he could see my dark, puckered rim now, see the quivering entrance to the passage I wanted him to fill.

Yes. I could not deceive myself, my desire was overwhelming. And after the long ride and my ponderings, I knew that to fight my need to be possessed by men would only ruin my life.

"Take me." I cried. "Plunge your great weapon into me and conquer me."

Konan laughed happily as his fingers played briefly with my rim; then one entered me. I moaned and whimpered, wanting more, wanting his huge manhood inside me. That huge legendary weapon that it was claimed could split a man not prepared for its entrance, but would also give unbelievable pleasure to any man who was ready and willing.

But the barbarian's fingers were as thick as many a man's weapon, and as long, and I moaned and panted as he stroked inside me with first one then two fingers, the entrance of that second one stretching me so that I let out a cry. Shortly, though, I was moaning for the way those fingers felt as they rubbed my spot. I was panting and dripping and writhing on the rug, trapped between his muscular thighs. But then Konan pulled my hips up and back, so that I was on my knees and my hand grasped my own tool and milked it.

"Yes," I cried. "Deeper," as Konan added a third finger to those playing inside my passage, causing me pain, but driving me wild till I was sending repeated spoutings of my seed across the rugs.

When I was spent, my head collapsed to the ground, and I lay there, limp, my ass still raised and Konan's fingers still playing inside it. They were no longer stretching and hurting me. I had accepted them, and opened for them, and they slid easily in and out of me. And I moaned my pleasure. Yes, this was the pleasure my nature desired almost above all other pleasures of the flesh.

The fingers left me then, and I whimpered at the loss, the emptiness. But then I cried out "Now. Let me feel your great weapon possess me, I am what I am. This is what I want." And I felt a great load lift off my shoulders, as I cried that to the trees, the river and the sky.

And I felt fingers pulling my cheeks apart again, but now an impossibly large club head was pressing at my entrance, and I willed myself to relax. Konan kicked my legs further apart, and his monstrous cock head was in the first way, and I felt I might burst apart, it truly was so large.

"You are too big" I cried, suddenly full of fear, "You are a giant, not a natural man. Ohhhh."

But the great barbarian did not withdraw, he pulled my hips higher and, with his knees, pushed my thighs even further apart, opening me wider, and that massive head moved in deeper. Making me pant and cry out as it made its slow progress, while I reached to take my own sword in my fist again. And I moaned and whimpered, and his weapon moved a fraction further into me as I began to stroke myself.

And as I did, I looked along up my body, to my hand working my stiffening weapon, and beyond I saw the great thighs of Konan between my spread legs, and I saw his balls hanging down. Full and heavy, covered in golden hair. What a sight, a glorious sight. If only I could see his weapon too, I thought. But only its root was visible as it was making its way painfully inside me, as I panted and moaned, and again cried out at how it was stretching and splitting me.

"Oh." I moaned, "Oh. No. It's too big."

But Konan never stopped. And however I moaned and cried out, I didn't want him to stop. For a while he was pressing and rubbing against that part of me that had my manhood throbbing and dribbling, and I moaned and whimpered as he pumped me there in short pulses, and I came. Spilling seed again, and again, across the rug.

Then he was some inches into me and I was bucking and arching, wanting him deeper, but feeling a stretching that was painful as he progressed into me.

It was some time before his great weapon had fully entered me. But finally he was in, and I felt the glossy golden hairs that surrounded his manhood rubbing against my asshole. Felt the touch of his huge balls. And I moaned in ecstasy. Yes, this was the greatest pleasure I had ever known.

But, no. Then the powerful barbarian stood up holding my hips to his, his sword in me still, and I spread my legs and wrapped them about his as wide as I could and he placed a hand under my belly and lifted me and moved my body back and forth, so that I fucked myself on his great club. My body limp and nothing but a toy for him, as he made the fucking deeper.

Then he leaned back against a nearby tree and turned me on his club so that I was lying back and looking up at him. What a magnificent sight he was. He was buried deep inside me, but he pulled my face to his so that his tongue could occupy my mouth in a rough, wet kissing.

Then he was moving me back and forth, going in and out, and I saw at last that great thick club he had impaled me on, as it come out of me, and then it was driving in again and I screamed as the sight of it had frightened me. But again I saw that steel-hard, fiery club partly emerge, and again he drove it back, deeper. But now I only moaned and arched back, as I knew I had taken it and I wanted more of it. It touched and explored every part of my channel, and I was in paradise.

Konan's weapon moved in and out of me until it was noon, and then he threw his head back and roared as he shuddered and jerked, and I felt his hot seed flood me as his throbbing tool delivered it deep inside me.

"Oh," I cried, overcome by the feel of it, that being a pleasure I had previously denied myself. "Oh, never before, never before. You are flooding me." No never before had I felt a man's seed flood me as Konan's did, and never since have I felt anything like it again. His seed was as prodigious as his organ was large.

For three days, each time we stopped to rest the great barbarian took me, and worked his club inside my ass. And we slept that way, him buried in my now well-stretched channel. A channel that never wanted to be empty. That can now take any man, of any size.

But when he had delivered me to my father, the Grand General, Konan was given his freedom. And he smiled at me, but then turned away, and without a backward glance strode proudly out of the Great Mogul's palace, out into the sun and fresh air of freedom.

And now that I am a man who knows himself, and what he is, and has no fear of it, I understand men of courage and how to lead and to inspire them. So that I have become a general also, almost as high as my father, the Grand General is. And I take my place at the head of the Great Mogul's armies now, just one step behind my proud father.

Book Two

Journeys Begin

Journeys Begin 1

I didn't look back. I may have rescued the Grand General's favorite son, Prince Kasim, from the Mongol raiders, but I knew that the Great Mogul's Grand General had no liking for me, and I saw it clearly in his slitted eyes as he gave me my freedom.

No. I did not look back or hesitate but instead strode out of that fine marble palace and onto the wide paved road and turned toward the east. I knew that I had traveled to the west as far as I wished to go, Now I headed east. Toward the sea. Toward the peoples of the islands in the ocean. Toward the land of the great river Nile, with its wondrous stone temples and tombs.

One day I would head further to the east and north, I knew, as in the end we will all long to return to somewhere that matters deeply to us. Ahhh, yes. But that day had not yet arrived. And now that place was too far away across the sea and the dusty mountains and more leagues distant than I cared to think on, for I had traveled far since leaving it and seen many wonders and met many men. But that place was my beginning, my true home.

* * * *

I realized what it was I wanted on the day I stood hidden outside the partly open door in a stone passageway of that far away place. As I stood there and watched old Timon take Cedric.

I had been looking for Cedric, who had gone off some time before and not returned. And I was moping about in search of him, as I loved nothing better than to be in his company, to watch his masculine and beautiful pale body move, to hear his voice, his laughter. To gaze into his deep blue eyes. To have him touch me as he did at times when helping me to relieve myself as a young man must, as I could not yet relieve myself easily with my hands still wrapped in bandages. I was young, barely a man. And I was still very innocent.

In my searching I finally heard the murmur of voices and, I confess, I walked softly and quietly along the passage to the open door ahead, from where they came. And outside the half-closed door I stopped, curious to know what they talked of. But what I heard was not serious talk of history and places far away, or even sensible words. What I heard was begging and sighs, and I moved closer to the door and looked in between the door and the frame on the side where the hinges were, sure I was hidden. I should have been ashamed, behaving so, but I was still a foolish uncertain youth.

What I saw through that crack held me fixed there almost afraid to breath. The old man, Timon, was kissing Cedric on the mouth, and his hands were lifting the thick woolen shirt from my friend's body. Cedric was begging, and moaning, "Yes, oh. Timon. Touch me. Yes. Oh. I want you so." And his own hands were roaming about Timon's thin shoulders and to his waist and disappearing inside the folds of his black woolen robe.

They pressed their bodies together then and embraced, wrapping their arms about each other as men and women do, and moving against each other, before pulling slightly apart. Then Cedric lifted Timon's robe, and in one swift movement had pulled it up and over his head and tossed it aside. The old man stood there naked now, his skin white and almost transparent with blue veins snaking about his sinewy and bony frame. I had seen few old men so naked and it both repelled and fascinated me. He was turned from me so I could not see his bush and his organ, which I was curious about. But Cedric then fell to his knees before the old man and Timon clasped at the thick black curls on my young friend's head and looked down. And we both watched as Timon's half hard manhood was lifted to Cedric's parted lips and I saw the end of it disappear into Cedric's mouth. Cedric's eyes closed as he slid his lips back and forth over the still half-soft organ. By this time my own manhood was well on the way to hardness, and I had lifted my robe and grasped it between both my bandaged hands.

My frustration raged inside me as my own rod grew harder and bigger than I think it had ever been before and began to throb, and I was so restricted by the bandages in bringing myself to my seeding. What I was seeing was driving me wild, and I knew that all I wanted was for it to be my weapon that was sunk in Cedric's mouth. My far larger manhood, growing bigger I was sure, since I had arrived at the temple, that moved back and forth between his full lips. With difficulty I stifled my groans as I spouted my juice in great bursts against the wood of the door.

And, as I did, Timon moaned and rolled his head about, and even I could see that his old organ was harder and longer now. Then he pulled himself from Cedric's mouth and tugged the young man to his feet and again they embraced and kissed as Cedric rubbed his belly from side to side against Timon. And again I wished it were me. That it was my hard manhood pressed to my own firm, flat belly that was being rubbed by Cedric's belly and hard tool. For I had no doubt he was hard too and I longed to feel the size and weight of his manhood in my hand. Oh, if only I had my hands free.

Cedric himself pulled the light robe he still wore off over his head as Timon looked on before running his hands over the younger man's pale-skinned flat belly and muscular chest. His fingers wrapping about the dark nipples and twisting and tugging at them as Cedric moaned, "Ohhh. Yes, Timon. Oh, yes. I am ready for you. Enter me," as they fell into another kiss.

I was still ignorant of what Cedric was asking for, but I came again, my hands doing what they could to my own organ, grown to throbbing need, at the sight of Cedric, naked, and being handled by Timon. I was young and in high heat and came often, and came so often that day I ached afterwards.

"Turn and show me your beautiful ass," Timon said, and Cedric turned and moved a step forward so he could lean over and rest his chest on the table where Timon had his clay tablets spread out. He was poised there with his legs spread, and as I watched, he reached back his hands and parted his ass cheeks and exposed his hole. I saw black hair in his crease and about his dark-rimmed hole and watched with rising heat as Timon reached for a pot on his desk and dipped his fingers into it and then pushed one finger into Cedric's asshole. His other hand I observed was stroking his own weapon as to my amazement the shiny fingers were poked deep into Cedric's hole. And I almost collapsed at the sight. First one finger, then two, then to the sound of Cedric moaning a third was added and Timon moved them in and out as Cedric's hips began to move with him, as if trying to have those fingers go deeper with each thrust. I came again and hardly stopped myself from falling against the door as my knees went weak.

"Deeper, deeper," Cedric moaned loudly.

Timon withdrew his fingers and grasped a short, round wooden object from his desk. I had seen it there often and thought nothing of it, but now he held the thick lump at one end and dipped the tip of its other, long, rounded end into the pot and it came out shiny and I realized the pot held oil. Then Timon was pressing it to Cedric's asshole, and it glided it as Cedric moaned with pleasure.

"More, more. Fuck me deep," he moaned, and Timon did drive the tool in deeper, but then drew it out of his ass. Timon moved it in and out for some time, then he withdrew it, and I saw he was now pressing the knob of his own hard manhood to the hole that now looked well oiled and more open, and old Timon's weapon slid into it easily.

I watched as his old cheeks clenched and bounced back, clenched forward and bounced back, as he pumped himself inside Cedric's channel.

Cedric moaned and moved his ass back and forth, matching Timon's stroking and making the old man's thrusts go deeper. "Oh, oh," Cedric moaned, and I saw one of his hands move to his own organ where it bounced beneath him and wrap around it and begin to stroke.

Timon pulled out and grasped a larger wooden rod, thicker and longer than the first and plunged it into Cedric's hole and pumped it strongly till Cedric jerked and spouted his manly seed out beneath him in big spurts. Then he returned his own organ to Cedric's ass canal and plowed him for some time before he bust into a frenzy of wild pounding that ended with him suddenly jerking to a stop and quivering, before collapsing over Cedric's back and wrapping his arms about him and kissing him. I soon realized this signaled Timon's own seed spouting inside Cedric

I left hurriedly on shaky legs and managed to reach my small room, where I looked at my own engorged manhood before I threw myself down and fucked into my bedding until I came twice more. I knew that my weapon was as long and thick, or larger even, than the second, thicker, wooden tool Timon had worked inside Cedric. And I knew that Cedric would moan more loudly for what I could give him than for anything Timon could do for him. And I knew that all I wanted to do was to see and feel Cedric's ass channel embracing my manhood as I pumped it in and out of him.

* * * *

Cedric. I knew I'd had strange feelings for him since I first saw him. Feelings I knew were not acceptable back in my village. Feelings such as I'd had for my friend, Rinon, before he drowned in the flooded pool, as I tried uselessly to save him. Feelings I had never done anything about but had pushed

111

aside, understanding they were not allowed among my people and knowing what it meant to be an outcast among my tribe.

And I knew that was much of why I had left my village and begun my travels. I had understood enough of myself to know that there was no happy place for me there. When Rinon drowned, my grief was tolerated but after several moons was seen by some to be as unnatural as my lonely brooding. I had all the advantages a youth could have in that place and time and my father was the head man of our village, and clever and understanding, just and fair. I was his eldest son and well made and strong and clever also. But after Rinon was gone, I grew to know that when I had been to my initiation in the hills, I would not be content to return and take the young woman Cleis, who was chosen for me, back to my parent's hut to be my wife and to live as I saw the other young men of the village live.

I had never touched Rinon in any way that was not acceptable, but he had filled my days as young men often fill each others. But—but there had been more, deep inside me there had been more, and my grief at his loss was deep. And for Cleis I felt nothing, and neither she nor any other village girl appealed to me at all.

It was my foolishness that had taken me there to the old stone temple high up the mountain. My foolishness could have killed me. But instead it had brought me there to that place far to the east and the north of where I was, and the men I found there were the making of me as a man.

* * * *

I had shivered uncontrollably, my teeth rattling together as I hugged my thin woolen cape tightly about me. Snow. It was all around me. And me in no more than my loincloth and the thin woolen cape my mother had woven for me, and with my weapons strapped to my back. My father's sword that would have been mine when I went for my initiation, the sheath and leather straps my brother had made for me, and the bow and arrows I had made for myself, which my young sister

112

had fletched for me. That was all I had to protect me in a world of snow blowing on a wind so cold it was like knives slashing at my skin.

I could not see anything but white. Blinding white. I knew that I was lost and that this body of mine that I was so proud of was almost at the end of its ability to survive. I remember letting out a wild howl of mindless anguish. Then I bent my head down and wrapped the cape about my mouth to warm the air that was freezing my lungs. And I breathed.

My body shook uncontrollably as I moved one foot in front of the other, unsteadily. I would not stop. I knew I could not lie down. So I moved. Moved with the fear of death upon me. Staggering in what my body told me was the right direction. Having nothing else to guide me

And I continued to place one foot in front of the other, until I no longer understood what a foot was. Or knew what walking was. Soon I no longer knew my own name, or if I was still alive. But still my feet somehow dragged me through the snow. Then the ground beneath me started to firm, though I did not know it, as I was now completely lost to the world about me.

* * * *

"Snow? That is snow?" I had asked just the afternoon before.

So young and foolish, sure I could overcome anything. Ah, yes, I was so very young still, and had not long left my home in the dry low hills further to the north.

"Yes, my young friend. That white stuff you see shining up high on the mountain is snow. Water made solid by the cold," Melioc the trader replied, smiling down at me as he rode upon his horse, with me, a foolish young Konan, walking at his side.

"No! Ha! Water cannot be solid." I exclaimed, sure he was making some joke with me.

"I am telling you the truth, Konan."

113

"Hard water? Is it some magic? For what reason would the gods make water solid?" I cried, turning such a strange idea as snow about in my mind and still not entirely believing it. But I also knew that Melioc was not a man to lie and one who had traveled widely and seen many strange and wonderful things.

"I do not think the gods have anything to do with it," Melioc replied, with a laugh at the strange question, I, the young barbarian who had been traveling with his caravan for ten days now had asked.

I was fortunate that when I left the hills of my home I had chosen to take the same road Melioc traveled and had soon come upon him and his two ox-drawn carts with their loads of fine wool. And I had greeted him and his five men as I had been taught to greet potential friends. Melioc had returned my greeting and questioned me in a language I hardly understood, but soon was speaking myself. Then when he knew who I was, he had said I could travel with them if I was willing to help with the heavy work and to guard the caravan if it was attacked. I had agreed easily. It was only several days before that I had left my village, but already I felt that the great world was mine and that I was destined to do great things in it. And Melioc traveled toward the great water. The sea, men called it. And that was my first goal. To see the sea.

"It does not look far," I had replied, looking up at the hills that rose up beside the trail, especially the higher one to our left, which had the most white on its slopes. "I shall see this wonder, I think, and see if it is as you say."

"The snow is far away, and the air is colder as you go higher up into the hills," Melioc warned me. "You do not have warm clothing or boots, Konan. It is a dry, sunny day down here today, but it is dangerous on the hills. Where there is snow, the weather can change quickly. In minutes it can turn from bright sunshine into a black storm. And there is little shelter on the mountain, and no one but the wise men live up there," he said, looking down at me seriously. Then he pointed up. "See that small dark spot? That is the place where the wise and holy men live."

Melioc pointed, and I followed his arm and saw a small, black mark set against the white of the snow, about half way up the mountain. But it was of no interest to me.

"Hum. I am decided. I shall see this wonder for myself," I replied stubbornly, even more determined to go now that Melioc, whom I greatly admired, implied I was not fast, or strong, enough to see it, "And it is far, but I am strong and fast and I shall easily climb to where the snow is and return to the road here in the light of one day," I boasted to him, determined to prove my courage and prowess to him.

"Pah. Put this idea from your head, Konan. I have come this way many times and heard many stories, and this is not a place to risk your life on a whim. You are young and strong, but the cold cares nothing for that; it will eat into you as if you were a shaking old grandfather who huddles by the fire all day."

"I am Konan. I am not some weakling," I replied heatedly. "I shall leave in the morning, at first light. And I shall climb the mountain and see this snow magic for myself, then I shall rejoin you on the next day," I added, knowing that we were almost at the place where Melioc was to set up camp for the night.

Ahh, to be so young and foolish. To have all my life before me still. Ha.

But of course Melioc was right. About all things. I reached the first snow that lay on the ground and discovered, when I held it in my hand, that it had a fiery bite to it but that it soon turned to water and ran through my fingers. It was a great wonder and I could see the peak of the mountain above me and the sun still not at its highest point. And about me I saw into the distance past many lower hills and over valleys, and I wondered what I might see if I climbed higher perhaps to the top of the snow covered mountain even. If I might from there see the sea that men talked of, or my home. What a wonder that would be. To stand on top of the world and see my home and the sea together. So, I climbed higher, full of energy and wonder. After climbing for some time in sun and warm air, my feet felt the chill coming through my sandals, and then, dark, almost green clouds rapidly rolled over me and brought a wind. I hesitated on my climb and turned and found I could not see the bottom of the mountain now, for it was hidden by other clouds. Then it had started to snow, and soon the wind was colder than anything I could have even imagined.

* * * *

Pain. My body was a mass of pain. Burning. My mind, foggy. To move was painful. I gasped, my lungs feeling raw. Things. There were large heavy things moving beside me, burning me where they touched me. And I was covered.

That is what I first clearly remember, being covered. And I let out a cry. A cry that sounded like no human cry, but a death rattle, as I thought that I was buried. That I had died. And had not traveled to the land of the dead as I should, but was trapped there, on the mountain, with the snow covering me forever. Terror of that endless afterlife of the lost cleared my head and reawakened my mind. I struggled to move my body, as if I could escape the clutches of my cold, lonely grave. But instead I felt more pain. Terrible burning pain, and I lost touch with the world again, for some time.

The next time I awoke I was shivering. Uncontrollably. But I could feel my limbs, and with confusion I saw that it was not snow that covered me but some fur. Light came in under the edge of the hide, not far above my eyes, showing a row of uneven hairs along its edge.

I lifted my trembling hand to my face and felt nothing but moved my arm and felt my warm breath on it and realized that the rawness had partly gone from my lungs, and I breathed more easily in spite of my terrible shaking.

But suddenly my confusion increased. A voice spoke nearby, and I did not understand what it said. I wondered if it was even human. But I tried to cry out at hearing it. I wanted to know where I was, and if I lived. My voice croaked and I could not make words, I shook so much. But then the fur was turned back, and I saw a face, one wrinkled and worn and dark. An old face that peered out of darkness at me. And I thought it was some demon of the gods, but then the mouth smiled, and I knew. I knew with no doubt, that it was human, and the fear fell away from my mind.

I lived. I lived. Ahh. Just to know that, when you have thought you are dead, is a bliss beyond imagining. "I am alive," my mind cried.

The face disappeared, and the fur was turned back over me. I was covered again, and voices murmured around me, and I must have slept. Then again the fur was removed and the light pained my eyes and I could hardly see. But I discerned that the room was dim anyway and only the brightness of a fire burning was clear to me. But the face was there again, and I was given a cup to drink from by an old, dry hand, which tipped its contents to my lips for me to drink. The liquid burned my mouth, and I shook so, but with the next mouthful, the pain was less, and when I finally swallowed the last of the stuff, I drank it almost easily. I lay back then and was covered with the furs and slept.

When I woke next, I remembered the snow and walking. And I shivered less and the pain was fading and becoming only a burning heat. On each side of me was a furnace that moved, and soon I realized that they were the bodies of large creatures that lay against me beneath the furs. And they gave me the heat I needed to rejoin the world.

I felt them there, firm and hot. The creature on one side I soon realized was covered in coarse thick hair. Always there. On the other side . . . that creature was smooth but then it was also rough haired and came and went, and at times I thought I only dreamed it and at times I thought it was a man, at others a beast.

I was made to drink frequently, and often it was a strange-tasting brown stuff I drank, and gradually I saw the room more clearly. It was small and had little but a fire and the pallet on which I lay. The old man had come and held a jar beneath my manhood and I understood, and filled it. Then I slept fitfully, and soon when I woke, I felt my manhood grown and firm as it is often, and I knew that I needed to find release.

My hand moved to my weapon, and a horror overcame me. No hand found my stiff weapon, only something soft, which pushed my manhood about. And my hand, I felt it, but it seemed to not do my will. I tried to open my fingers but could still not reach my tool and I felt a new fear. A fear of the unknown, of a dozen barbarian horrors. Of having no hands now, of not being able to move my body of . . . of a dozen such things I knew I could not live with. I had thought the pain in my body bearable, and my hand warm, if stiff. But it was not so, though I struggled still to grasp my manhood.

Then a hand wrapped itself about my engorged weapon and I sighed in relief. But my relief was short-lived as I quickly knew it was not my own hand that encircled and ran up and down my hard length. I was shocked to discover that one of the creatures lying by me now was touching me so. And his hands felt like a man's hand and he stroked me well, and I moaned and my hips moved voluntarily, aiding the action of the hand. I ached for release, but when my seed left me it was not in its usual wild bursts, and my heat was quickly gone.

The man lying against me had felt hot and solid and had a rich scent to him. I was embarrassed and confused at what had happened, but I was also too tired to brood on any of this and slept again instead.

I awoke to find myself alone under the furs and apart from soreness in my fingers and toes I was no more than achingly tired and my belly gnawed at me with hunger. And I was hard again. I felt my belly rumble as I reached uselessly for my throbbing tool and moaned quietly in frustration and fear.

I knew I must know the worst and I turned aside the furs covering me and held my arms up and looked at where my hands should be. I cried with relief that they were not gone but also with fear at what lay hidden inside the brown, oily, wound fabric that covered them, turning them into useless lumps.

That cry of fear and uncertainty brought my carers hurrying to me.

There were two of them there then, living alone in that big stone temple on the side of the mountain and I was told there was a third, who was away fetching provisions. And they told me that the great course-haired creature that lay against me at night, warming me, was the dog, Lycos. My carers were two old men, but both were tall and lean, with silver hair, and when they were not covered entirely by their heavy flowing black capes and hoods, they were fine looking elders. But one was losing his wits to the gods, and often when I saw him he sat gazing sightlessly into the distance and not moving. Then he suddenly laughed a dry, short laugh, then smiled and mumbled. But sometimes he would recite to me also. For he had been a reciter, a man such as a traveling singer is, a bringer of news and tales from far away. But now he seemed to remember only one tale, and if he began to recite then it was always to name the fallen in some great battle.

I first heard him reciting when I had been in the temple for at least ten days. I was awoken by the sound of his voice, as he stood inside my door looking down at me, and most of what he said I understood, though many of the names sounded odd to the tongue.

" . . . Meanwhile Meriones killed Phereklos, son of Hermonides, a man who knew all manner of building arts and handicrafts. . . overtaking him, Meniones hit his buttock on the right and pierced his bladder, missing the pelvic bone. He fell, moaning upon his hands and knees and death shrouded him. Then Megas killed Pedaios, bastard son of Lord Antenor . . ." he recited in a voice that made me listen. He continued on for some time, listing how men died, and I did not interrupt him though there seemed something of the spirit of the dead about him.

Later when Timon, came to me with the draught I had to drink thrice daily to help my body heal,I asked him what battle it was Armenis told of.

Timon replied, "He remembers the great battle of Troy, where so many of the finest of Troy and Greece died, that no one who was there can ever forget it."

119

"I know nothing of this battle," I said, for I loved to hear the tales of battles told by traveling bards. "Why was it fought?"

"For a woman, Helen, men say. But really it was fought for a king's pride, for the loyalty of brothers, and for the duties our Greek kings owe to each other to keep the peace between them."

"Ha. That sounds foolish." I replied, "My people would not fight for anything but our own land and homes."

"Then you are young and fortunate, Konan. And it was many years ago, and far away to the east," Timon replied, "When Armenis and I were still young men."

The first day I had recovered enough to be almost myself in my mind, Timon had discovered he could talk with me in a rough version of the tongue the merchant Melioc had spoken.

He was a wise man, was Timon. His companion of the fading mind, Armenis, he said had once been as fit and clever as him, and they were of an age, having seen seventy-eight summers come and go. And Timon told me that many moons had passed over their heads, and many leagues of the earth had passed beneath their feet before they had finally come to rest in the old abandoned temple on the side of the mountain.

There were times later when I saw Armenis look up at nothing, and snarl and wave his arms and yell incoherently. If Timon was about he was silent then.

Almost half a moon passed before I was able to walk about and I was stiff and sore as I had never been before. It was Timon who made the brown spicy soup and brought it to me in that small hot room. I had to drink it several times a day, but once I was recovered enough to feed myself the soup he brought, I was allowed to stand up and walk stiffly on my bound feet out of that small room. And I was sure I was suddenly growing again also, taller and stronger, which pleased me, but my hands and feet were still encased, and I wanted to see my hands, and my feet, to be sure they were all right still.

But Timon said, "No. You must wait for them to heal," so I asked what had injured them, and he said, "The cold."

I shivered at the memory of that white blinding cold and asked no more,but said,"I shall go soon. As soon as I am fit to walk down the mountain. For I have a journey to undertake." As I was already pacing all about the temple restlessly, eager for more activity, with my feet tender and sore but bearing my weight. Timon fixed his dark, deep-set eyes on me. " No. It will be nearly two moons and spring will be near before your hands and feet have healed enough for you to safely walk from this mountain, and you will need the healing soup till then," he said.

Never having been ill or hurt in any real way before, I did not believe him and wanted to be on my way again. "Old man, I am grateful to you for your care, but I am young and strong and my legs can carry me again. So I shall leave as soon as you can take these coverings from my hands and feet," I replied with the arrogance of youth.

He fixed me with his eyes again. "No. If you refuse to listen to me, I shall unwrap your hands and feet, and you shall be a cripple all your life."

I was angry with him, but afraid too of what he said. For I also half believed he was some weaver of magic also. So, instead of fighting him I walked away to sulk. And I unwound part of the bandaging on one of my hands, just enough to see dead white matter peeling off the raw new flesh that lay beneath it, and I hurriedly rewound the bandage. That place has never healed so well as the rest, and to this day it reminds me of Timon's wisdom.

Then late the next morning, as I brooded increasingly on the wrongs of my situation, a young man of wonderful appearance arrived at the heavy wooden doors leading into the temple. He entered the courtyard with an ox-cart loaded with provisions, and accompanied by a great dog, similar to the one named Lycos that lived in the temple and warmed me at night, which bounded in to greet me.

"I have returned," the young man called out, as he entered the courtyard and I looked up from my brooding and keeping his great dog at bay to better see this new arrival.

He had thrown off his hood now and I saw a tall, handsome dark-haired man, of good height and strong build. His body was well wrapped in a robe such as Timon and his companion wore but even that could not hide his strength.

I walked out to greet him, curious. "So you are up and about," he said as soon as he saw me. "You look well on Timon's potion. And your hands, they do not pain you?" he asked me, taking hold of one of my bandaged hands gently with both his hands and turning it about.

As he did this, I noticed that he was missing his smallest finger on one hand and the first joint of a finger on the other. "All looks well. Good. You will not lose anything as I did," he said raising his hands for me to see the missing joints clearly.

"Do you mean that you lost your fingers from the cold?" I asked him, shocked.

"Yes. Like you, I was too long in the cold, but I wasn't so lucky and did not stumble on this temple before I collapsed to die. Instead, it was the great dog Anubis, brother to Lycos, and my constant companion, who found me half buried in the snow and saved me."

And he threw back the hood of his heavy black robe and pointed at his nose. "See here? And these, my ears?" his pointed to the tip of his nose and his ear lobes.

All were not as smooth or long as they should be. And his face, which would otherwise have been wonderfully handsome, was made rough and uneven by the losses. But in spite of this damage, this friendly giant's body was still immensely handsome and gave off an attractive animal warmth and strength such as no other man I had ever met before.

"The gods have smiled on you, young Konan," he said, himself smiling beautifully on me, me a foolish, ignorant, young barbarian.

"You know my name?" I replied annoyed, "And what is yours?"

"I am Cedric," he said, "and I live here. And now, young Konan, you can help me to unload this cart."

Journeys Begin 2

I knew instinctively that it was Cedric who had gripped my manhood and milked it for me as I lay between life and death in those first days. I had never thought it was Timon's thin body that had lain beside me when it felt like a man beside me, rather than a rough haired beast. I will confess that I had since wondered if I had imagined it all, though I longed to feel again that large firm hand encircle me and give me the release I now struggled to get alone.

I could hardly take my eyes from Cedric, and yes, my manhood acknowledged him. I wore a thick, warm, but well-worn robe of Timon's and was blushingly grateful that my now-stiff rod was hidden as we worked. Or so I thought. For when we were nearly finished with unloading the wagon, Cedric said, " I see that you are glad I have returned," and smiled at me.

And I blushed more, much to my embarrassment, but I replied boldly, surprising myself, "Yes, he remembers you. For it was you who relieved him for me in those first days, wasn't it?"

Cedric looked at me differently. "Yes, my young barbarian, it was I who took Anubis place and lay with you," he said quietly. "And I who gave you the other also, for at times a young man needs release as much as anything else."

"I thank you," I replied, suddenly uncertain of what I wanted to say, knowing I wanted to again feel his firm large hand encircling me and sliding, oh sliding . . .

That night I lay down on my pallet in a turmoil. My head was full of Cedric. I had ogled him all day and followed

124

him about, helping him as much as I could with my bandaged hands to carry and store the supplies and carry out work not done while he was absent. For he was the fittest and strongest one of them, and they were very dependant on him, I discovered, learning that he served the two old men and studied with Timon.

It was Cedric who went into the world to gather provisions and who hunted game with the great dogs Lycos and Anubis. Though apparently it was but only one season since Timon had still accompanied them on the hunt.

So, that night I sighed and slid my manhood between my bandaged hands and, frustrated at the inadequacy of that, rolled over and rubbed back and forth against the furs beneath me. And in spite of my panting and moaning, I still heard the heavy door of my small room creaking open softly.

"I thought you could use some help," Cedric said, and before I knew what he meant, he had joined me on my pallet and pushed me on my side and grasped my manhood in his strong hand.

I moaned in ecstasy at the feel of him and pressed myself against him, feeling the solidness of his body through this robes and scrabbling at them uselessly, trying to undress him so that I could feel his skin, his heat, his body against my skin. Ahhhh. I longed to run my hands down his belly, longed to taste him. My mouth was open, panting, and needed to be filled.

But . . . Cedric pulled away.

"I must go," he said, his voice rough.

"No, no," I cried out. "Stay," I begged him, and if my hands could have, I would have grabbed him and held him there.

But he left me seething with frustration and desire, and when I saw him again, he was cool with me, and I knew I had offended him. And he did not come again to help me find release as he had before. So now I raged to Timon that my hands and feet were still not healed enough for me to leave that place.

"Patience," Timon said.

But I had no patience and I was sure I had offended the man whose companionship I wanted most.

* * * *

Ahh, Cedric. In the beginning he was a giant—though not as large as I am now—and I was but a lean and strong young barbarian. I bowed to no man, but like a young puppy will the one who feeds him, I worshipped Cedric, from our first meeting. And in truth I have still not met a man to equal him.

So, I took my pride in hand and told Cedric that I begged his forgiveness for what offence I had caused him. It was the first time I bowed my head as a man and asked forgiveness of another and one of the few times I ever have.

He said, "There was no offence, young Konan, but . . . but you are young, and there is much you do not understand." He would say no more

Then I followed him about and was of some use to him as he did what work about the place had gone undone while he was away but also hindered him often, for I knew nothing of the work needed to keep a stone and timber building in order. So, he gave me the duty of feeding the great dogs Lycos and Anubis and taking them out into the snow beyond the temple walls. I found then that Timon was right and that, even well wrapped, my feet ached badly after only a short walk on the cold of the snow. But as days passed, we began to return with small game, and as I healed, I began going down the mountain farther, but not as far as the end of the snows.

At other times I followed Cedric to the rooms of the temple where Timon sat and bent over lumps of dried clay. Such a foolish thing to do, I thought, and I said as much to the old man one day.

"Why do you bend over what is nothing but hard earth?" I said to him as he studied the flat tablet he held in his hand.

126

"You see only what you understand, Konan," he replied gently, looking me in the eye as he always seemed to when he told me thing of importance. So I was quiet.

"If you look properly at the surface of this tablet, you will see marks in even rows, marks not made by nature," he said and, wrapping an arm about my shoulders, drew me to him and pressed me against his thin old body and I looked at what he held and followed his finger tip as it traced strange sharp marks across its surface.

"These marks tell me that Armenis and I went to the great city of Babylon where there were many gardens. And the king had many slaves, of which 500 worked in the palace and its grounds."

"Ha! How can it tell you that?" I asked him, thinking that, like Armenis, Timon too was now losing his mind in his old age.

But his finger traced out the marks and he said, "Here, these mean garden. And these mean 500, and this, slaves," he said. "Do you see the patterns, Konan? See the letters that make the words?"

I could see some pattern in what he pointed at, but that proved nothing.

But he pulled another tablet from the pile he had and pointed again, and I saw that where he pointed, one of the patterns was repeated, "What pattern is this?" he asked me.

"500," I replied, still thinking it a strange coincidence only.

But he pulled yet another tablet out and again pointed to the pattern. I was a barbarian and used to discerning the patterns of animal tracks on the ground and the patterns of stars in the sky, and to see a simple pattern of shapes cut cleanly into clay was no great effort.

I looked at him and at the tablets scattered about—so many of them. "So, they tell you some king had 500 slaves. Do they tell you where to find them, or how many warriors he had?" I asked, curious now.

Timon laughed. "It tells me many things. How many soldiers, yes, and whom we met and what strange gods they worshipped."

"But there are many tablets," I said, frowning now and wondering how much might be told on them.

"Armenis and I traveled far in search of wisdom," he replied, smiling. "Even as far as the holy Nile, where the great crocodiles swim."

"And where are these places, this Nile and this Babylon with the gardens?" I asked, thinking that they must be close by and might be worth my visiting on my way to the sea.

"Far away across the ocean," he replied. "Over the sea, which is endless salt water and full of great dangers."

"I have heard of the sea," I said proudly. "And one day I shall go there and travel over it. One day I shall cross the ocean and see what lies there. I shall find this place with twenty gardens and this king with 500 slaves and this Troy where the men Armenis tells of died."

I had heard of the ocean and I already intended to conquer it, but I had no idea then how great the world was, and yet how small. Nor how many oceans there might be. But I did find the ruins of the palace that once had many gardens and have traveled to the sacred Nile, to the land of the Great Mogul and many other places where great armies battled and great and wondrous cities fell.

"Perhaps you will," Timon replied, smiling and laughing at me indulgently. "Then you too may want to write your story for others to read."

"Show me how to write," I said, "show me," almost excited now.

Timon took up a tablet of wet clay for a barrel of water that sat below the table then picked up a pointed stick. "So, what shall I write?" he asked me.

I thought for a moment. "The week before my initiation into manhood, I, Konan, left my village to discover the great world. On the first day . . ." I said telling him the very beginnings of my journey.

"Enough, enough." Timon cried, and using the sharp stick he made marks, letters he called them, in neat rows on the wet clay. "Here," he said when he had made many marks made a line and a half, "here is your name, Konan," he said pointing to one group of his letters.

I studied what he was showing me, and taking the stick from his hand, I copied my name into the clay. "One day I shall write my story," I said proudly.

He looked at me seriously then and said, "You learn quickly, Konan. Perhaps one day you will discover the great world and perhaps you will even write your story for men to read."

"Is Cedric also a wise man?" I asked him then, uncertainly.

"Cedric? Yes. He is very wise," he replied and then sat still looking at me. "But you mean is he like Armenis and I? Yes, he is." Timon replied. "In every way. Though you may not understand what I mean."

Timon returned to poring over his tablets, and I wandered off in search of Cedric. He was working in the kitchens with old Armenis watching him.

I was restless and did not want to be made to do woman's work in the kitchen. And it annoyed me that Cedric did. "Why do you do this, why are there no women here to prepare the food?"

"Because there are not," Cedric replied patiently.

The nights I spent alone I rubbed my belly and my organ raw on the fur on which I still slept, wetting it several times with my seed, which I spilled while thinking of Cedric's hands on me and mine on him, and of his body lying beside me. Ahhh, I was so frustrated, and each night I was ready to tear the bandages from my useless hands, stopped only by the thought of Cedric's missing fingers.

* * * *

Then came the day I saw Timon riding Cedric and returned to my room in heat, understanding now what I wanted from him, and raging that he wanted old Timon more than me.

It seemed like an omen that Timon came to my room very early the following morning, accompanied by Cedric, who was carrying a bowl of warm water and a pot of ointment and strips of fresh white linen.

"It is time to see how your hands and feet fare," Timon said.

"You will uncover them?" I cried ecstatically. "I will be able to use them again? I will be able to leave here?"

"No," he said sternly, "not yet. They will be bandaged again, but only lightly, and you will have more movement, if all is well."

For a moment I wanted to scream in frustration but held my tongue, as I knew I was also grateful to Timon for saving me. And I was torn, wanting to leave that place, but wanting Cedric also.

I held my hands out and rested them on the small table in the room, and he was slowly unwinding the cloth from them. Cedric looked on intently and occasionally looked up at me and smiled reassuringly, and it was all I needed to make my manhood throb and send all thoughts of leaving that place from my mind. I had such a desire to feel my flesh lying against his. To feel his hands encircle my manhood and stroke it for me.

My hands were healing well. Dead white skin fell away from them, and the raw, tender skin beneath even I knew needed protection for a while longer.

* * * *

Armenis went missing that same day. We had to let the dogs go to find him, and Timon was shaking with cold when we returned with an also shaking and struggling Armenis. He shouted about his mother and wanting to go home, and I saw

130

tears in Timon's eyes. Armenis was put to bed in their room and Timon sat with him and Cedric took them food and drink. In the night there were wild cries and the sounds of banging. In the morning Timon had a bandaged arm and seemed shaky and uncertain. Armenis stayed in their room and the door was kept barred.

"Has Armenis lost his mind to the demons now?" I asked Cedric as I ate my evening meal, for I had seen a woman in our village give her senses up to the demons and die for it soon after.

"He gets worse and better." Cedric replied.

"He is old," I said.

Now that I had good use of my hands I was thinking often of Cedric and of how I wanted to ride him. I was growing stronger and bigger, Timon had said it was the healing soup taken at the start of manhood that caused it. For I was growing faster than I ever had before, and it gladdened me that my manhood also grew and thickened along with my body.

"They have been together for over fifty years," he said angrily, "and Timon is also old. I doubt he will survive the loss of Armenis. Can you understand that?" he said angrily.

I thought of Rinon, and I said, "Yes I can understand it, but there is nothing you or I can do to help Armenis. His mind is with the spirits."

"But what of Timon? I would help Timon in any way I can," Cedric said, a look of anguish on his face that tore at me. For I understood finally in that moment part of what was between him and the old man, and also—yes I was still naïve—part of what had been between Timon and Armenis for all those years.

"So . . . so, Timon has lain with Armenis all these years?" I asked, slightly shocked.

Cedric looked at me in anguish. "Yes," he said in a whisper. "Yes."

"I have seen you with Timon," I said boldly. "I want you also, and my manhood is of a bigger size and thickness, and would satisfy you more. Why will you not lie with me

131

also?" I asked. Glad that I now understood some of what was happening about me in that place.

"Timon saved my life and has taught me all I know. He loves me and I him and I will do anything for him," he said angrily. "I owe him everything. I am his," he said, and hurried from the kitchen.

* * * *

Some weeks passed and at first Armenis improved, but then he began to wander again and had to be watched constantly or locked in his room.

"Konan," Timon called to me from across the small courtyard of the temple one day, and I came out of the small stable where the ox was kept to find him looking about and frowning.

"Cedric has told me that you have seen him and I together," he told me, looking me in the eye.

"Yes," I replied, and added boldly, "and I have told him I could give him my weapon, one that is bigger and stronger to pleasure him."

Timon looked at me closely. "You are not like Cedric," he said. "You will leave here gladly when you can, not feel a duty to stay."

"I will be grateful to you always for many things," I replied, "doubt that not, Timon. But I am a free man and the life of study and isolation is not for me."

"When we were young, it was not for Armenis and me either, Konan. Like you, we longed to see the world. Only when we were too old to travel roughly did we settle here to see our days out."

"Then why have you not told Cedric it is time he left you?" I asked.

"Because . . . because now we cannot get by without him. And because when he could have left, he refused to go, and, foolishly, we let him stay. But now Armenis is . . . is no longer Armenis, and life has grown meaningless to me." He paused, " In a few days your hands and feet will have healed and you will take Cedric away form here, but first . . . first you must take him as a lover; you must break the bond he believes he has to me. Show him what it is to be taken by a young man who has some love for him and can truly satisfy him. Do this, Konan, do it quickly, because in a few days it will be time for both of you to leave here. And he must go with you. He must go." As always when he was most serious Timon fixed me with his deep-set, dark eyes.

"I long to take him but he will not . . ."

"You must take him. By force if necessary. You are almost as strong as he is now, and far more cunning. Be gentle, if you can, but it must be done. Soon."

I had some feeling what was to come, but I did not bother to think on it. I had all I could want. Timon's order to take Cedric.

* * * *

I approached the taking of Cedric as I would any hunt, and as I was not allowed to fail, I thought on the best place and considered the best way. That I who was a virgin still should be planning such a thing would have made many laugh, but I had spent many weeks now thinking of all those things I wanted to do with Cedric. I had brought myself release innumerable times imagining me taking him and had forgotten nothing of the long fucking I had seen Timon give him.

The following morning I told Cedric that the big storeroom had rats in it, and he angrily hurried there. I followed behind him and when he entered the room and had gone behind the shelves, I slid the board across the door and took up the rope I had set there ready.

"Where did you see the rats?" he called out.

"Here among the empty jars," I said, standing near the empty wine jars, each one half as long as a man and perhaps a third as wide as a man is tall, that lay on their sides in the back of the room.

He hurried over and was bending and peering between them when I pushed him over on them He was too stunned to react before I had already tied both wrists together and to the neck of one jar and was tying his left ankle to the handle of another.

"What are you doing?" he cried out, and struggled. "Let me go. Are you mad?"

I ignored him, but it took all my strength to get his right ankle tied off to the handle of another jar so that his legs were spread wide, his body lying ass up along the middle jar. I was already stiffening, having been excited all morning, and the sight of him lying there at my mercy was all I needed to arouse me to the highest heat.

"Now you shall know what it is to be truly filled and satisfied," I said to him. "And this shall happen whether you want it to or not, for Timon has ordered it so," I added. It was cruel to say that, I knew, but I also thought it might quieten him. But it did not. He struggled wildly and shouted abuse at me and claimed I lied and that Timon loved him.

I knew it was best to ignore him and merely pulled his robe from him and revealed his long pale-skinned muscular back, his full round ass cheeks, and his spread legs. I stuffed his robe under his belly so his own manhood did not rub too much against the rough clay of the wine jars, and then I oiled up my fingers in the oil pot and moved between his spread legs, straddling the tapered end of the jar on which his body rested.

I was gentle with him. Well I tried to be. Ahh. Now I know that I was too wild and inexperienced to be even halfway as gentle as I should have been. Ahhhh, well.

I oiled him up and reached for his weapon and stroked that as well as I could as I worked my fingers inside his channel and opened him. And in spite of his continued protests, he began to grow and stiffen for me. When I thought I had done enough at his hole and could wait no longer anyway, I withdrew my fingers and, oiling my own rock hard and throbbing manhood, I pressed the head to his hole and with some difficulty entered him.

I moaned loudly and crying, "Cedric," I lost control immediately at the feel of his channel embracing and holding me. I slammed my hips into his ass, and he screamed, but I could not stop, and I plowed into him again, and a third time, and spilled my seed deep inside him. And I roared. A great roar of the wild joy of possessing him, and of release and taking.

When I had fisted his own still-firm weapon till he came himself I was ready again, and I filled his channel with my seed two more times before I withdrew my manhood from inside him and released him from the ropes. When I did, he fell to the ground and huddled up.

I knelt beside him and stroked his hair and held his hand and brought it to my mouth to kiss. "Timon says we must leave here soon. You and I," I said to him.

"No. No. I will never leave them," he cried, and I heard him sob. "I have been unfaithful. How could you . . ." he said, then pulled himself up and pulled away from me. "I hate you," he cried and ran off.

* * * *

Cedric avoided me then, but in four days my hands were unbandaged for the last time, and though the skin on my fingers looked pink and soft, it was fully healed. The next day Timon summoned us both to his writing room. He was looking frail and old and stooped now. In just a few weeks he had aged into an old man. The clay tablets were all neatly stacked up by the walls, the bucket beneath the table was dry and empty, and his table was clear. "You two must leave tomorrow. You will take the ox-cart and the dogs with you and go to the south. Konan wishes to travel to the sea, and it is as good a direction as any to head in."

"Why do you talk like this? I cannot leave you, and you cannot manage without me," Cedric cried, flying into a panic

"After tomorrow Armenis and I will have no need of any help you can give us," Timon replied in a steely voice. "The last thing you will do for us is to bury us before you go."

"No. No. But you are alive, what are you talking about? You have many years to live still."

"No! Cedric. Silence!" Timon shouted. "I have no desire to live past losing Armenis. And I have lost him. The man I have loved all these years is gone. Don't you see that?"

I had to pull Cedric away, as he was determined to stop Timon doing what it was he intended. And I pitied my friend, for I knew he truly loved the old man.

"Are you sure this is what is right? Cedric has a great love for you and you still have many years in you," I said

"This is what I want, and with Armenis gone I doubt I have more than a few painful months left in me," he replied, his eyes now deep and sorrowful.

I understood and argued no more.

* * * *

But Cedric. Poor Cedric; he had set a simple and good course to his life, and now all he had was being cut from under him. And he was falling, lost and shattered. I had chosen to leave my village and had no regrets, the temple only an unexpected stop along the way, while Cedric had found his home on that mountain and was being dispossessed.

I took him to his room, and we struggled hard, but finally I prevailed. And having won, I tied his hands to the frame of his bed and stripped his robe from him and again entered him, as he shouted at me to stop. And I fucked him long and hard until he gave up his cries and shouting, and instead he moaned for me, and arched and came before finally sinking back exhausted. And when he slept, I undid his hands and left him.

In the kitchen I found Timon stooped and shuffling. "The soup," he said, pouring the brown stuff I had been drinking all these months from a pot into a small wine jar and stoppering it. "Take it with you, Konan. Strength and size sit well on you, and while it lasts, this potion will continue to make you grow bigger, and stronger."

I looked on as Timon worked and watched as he ground more herbs up and shook them into a bowl and poured water over them. He looked down into the bowl for some minutes, then looked up at me, "I am done now," he said, with a sigh.

Instinctively, I moved to him for I was most grateful to him, and my mouth found his, and his mouth responded, and we embraced in silence. Then I pushed him back over the table, but he pushed me away. "No. No, Konan. You have never known what it is to be made love to. And you will never be a great lover of men if you do not understand what it is to have a man make love to your body, as you make love to him. Close your eyes and imagine I am young, that I am Cedric or some other young man you have admired. Do it," he ordered, and he found my lips in a kiss and I closed my eyes.

It was not hard to imagine he was some much younger man. He ran his hands over me—flutteringly at first, then firmly, his fingers brushing my nipples and sending little waves of pleasure through me before his fingertips ran over my belly and all about my body. Then it was his lips, sucking at my nipples, and his teeth, nipping them sharply, sending jolts of fire through me that made me gasp and jerk, then moving down, making my body sing as if touched by some spirit. I sought his nipples with my hands and rubbed and pinched them also. Then he moved his mouth down my body, tasting me, his tongue exploring each crease and hollow of me as it worked over my chest and down my belly to my manhood, my weapon already grown throbbingly hard again. His mouth engulfed me, and I moaned loudly, for the wonder of feeling that for the first time, and later because in his long life old Timon had learnt all there was to know of pleasuring a man. He made love to my manhood so that I cried out at the wonderful feeling of it and spouted my seed in his throat, and then he made love to it again and let it spout across his chest.

My eyes were open now, and I saw my cream settling in the gray hair that ran across his wiry chest, and I leant to lick it from him.

When I was hard again he lay back upon the table and his face was more relaxed and happy than I had ever seen it, and he had me oil my fingers and explained to me what spot gave a man the greatest pleasure as I fingered inside his rarely entered ass canal. Ahh, he taught me much. He had traveled the world and was a scholar who made love to many men, and there was little he did not know of the art. If I have learnt anything since that night, it was probably only because he forgot to show it to me.

I fucked him repeatedly, taking him deeply and strongly, or gently and shallowly as he instructed me, and I felt the wonder of the variety of the ways he had me do it. Ahh yes. He was a fine guide to pleasuring the body of man. And he moaned and sighed and arched for me and came. He came for me twice, and finally a third weak time. And when we had kissed deeply one last time, he took the bowl of soaked herbs to the room he shared with Armenis and closed the door.

After that final sight of him, I was tired but could not sleep. Timon had left the possessions I had arrived at the temple with cleaned and ready for me in my room, and I removed the heavy woolen robe I had grown accustomed to and again put on my loincloth, cleaned and made soft with oils but now barely covering me, I had grown so. And I put on my weapons, my father's sword and the bow and arrows I had made myself and that my sister had fletched for me, and I laced up my sandals and wrapped the light cloak my mother had woven for me about my shoulders, ready to continue my journey into the world.

Then I loaded all that was valuable in the old temple onto the ox cart before I went to prepare a meal. And with warm food in my belly, I began to dig their graves. The earth where Timon had told me to dig was in their small orchard, and it was hard but had been dug over well at the start of the previous autumn and covered with straw before the snow set in, and it was now thawing, for spring was well advanced.

When the sun was rising I woke Cedric.

* * * *

I didn't look back. But Cedric looked back many times after had we left the old temple and he was silent in the afternoon as we walked down the mountain beside the ox cart with the two great dogs, Lycos and Anubis, loping along ahead of us. And as I was sore and tired, the silence suited me well enough. That first night we camped at the place where Melioc had made his camp the night before I had gone up the mountain to see the snow for myself, and I wondered where the merchant was now and what he thought had become of the young barbarian, Konan, all those moons ago. And I wondered with amazement myself at how wild and innocent that young barbarian who had set off up the mountain had been.

In the night Cedric moved his body close to me, and I moaned in ecstasy at the feel of him and pressed myself against him, feeling the solidness of his body through his robes and scrabbling at them to undress him so that I could feel his skin, his heat, his body against my skin. Ahhhh. I longed to run my hands down his belly, longed to taste him. My mouth was open, panting, and needed to be filled. And fill it he did, by bringing his face to mine and sending his tongue into my mouth to duel briefly with mine. And my hands found his chest and it was finally pressed to my skin. My own healed hands able to pull him willingly to me at last.

And then I felt his manhood. And my mind became clouded with the heat of desire. His rod was hard and thick and pressed to my thigh, its heat feeding my own, and I pressed my thigh harder against it and spouted my seed up between us in strong spoutings.

His mouth left mine. And I bent my head. I had hands to feel his body now, and my mouth to taste him and my tongue to explore him, and I used all of them. I ran my tongue

139

down his body, feeling the hairs that grew about his chest and trailed down his belly to his bush and then my nose burrowed there, smelling him and feeling his manhood hard against my cheek until I was tasting it. Instinctively, my tongue found the swollen slitted head of him and lapped at it, tasting his juices. And as I had learned from Timon's example, I caressed and sucked on it. Cedric's hands tangled in my hair, and he moaned and whimpered and I applied my lips to his manhood again, wanting him to moan even louder for me and spout for me. And I had barely begun to follow the veins down and suck on them before he trembled and cried out and my mouth was full of his seed.

Then I turned him over onto his belly and lifted his hips up off the blanket he lay on and he reached back and parted his ass cheeks for me. Inviting me into him. I opened him with my fingers, making him moan and writhe and move his hips before I even gave him my manhood. Finally, I worked my weapon in him as I now knew how to do, so that it was not painful for him to take my weapon, which was already of uncommonly large length and thickness, and he arched and writhed and moaned and cried out wildly at my taking, which was so wonderful to witness, and I came inside him with a mighty roar. My first taking of a willing Cedric. The first of many.

* * * *

My thoughts returned from that long distant past, from the beginnings of my journey to the west, back to my present journey, where my steps were taking me back, back to the east. The road leading east from the Great Mogul's palace was busy, and I did not stop to do more than eat and sleep until I was near the end of the lands the Great Mogul controlled. I had walked for many days, and if my body had got soft in the Grand General's dungeons, it quickly became as hard and muscular as it had ever been and the sun gave me a darker color.

A moon had passed and another was nearly gone when I stood at the top of a low hill looking down at the road ahead of me. It stretched onward and wound among hills until it was lost to sight. And still it was busy. Goods and merchants coming to the richest lands I had seen in all my travels. The lands of the Great Mogul. But I was now far enough from his armies and his fine palaces to slow my pace, and I looked about me.

My eyes were drawn to the south, where I saw a large building, surrounded by fields of ripening grain, and I turned that way, for it was already late afternoon and I was tired of sleeping on the ground.

Servants scattered to hide as I approached the open entrance to the farm building, and walking through the wooden gates I entered a wide courtyard floored with hard packed earth and surrounded by the well-built stone walls of the large fortified farm house. It was silent except for a voice singing, and the singer was at the trough in the center of the yard. He was pouring water over himself from a hide bucket that he had drawn up from the well beside the trough. His head was tilted back, and the water was sluicing the dust and sweat from his young and lean, but athletic body. And he was a truly magnificent sight. Ahhhhhhhhhhh.

If I had not already known that it was too long since I had mastered a truly desirable man for my pleasure, the sight of him would have told me so immediately.

"I am weary from the road," I said loudly as I approached him.

He turned suddenly to me, as if surprised, and greeted me. "Welcome stranger." he said, looking me up and down with mixed shyness and desire. "I am Hilaron, son of Margaret, only daughter of Mortho, and my father is David. And . . . and I am master of this house . . ." he hesitated again, and his manhood I saw was growing, " . . . and if you come in peace, you are welcome."

"I come in peace," I replied.

142

Book 3

The Inheritance

Master of the House

As I bathed at the trough by the well in the courtyard, I sang a song my mother used to sing to me when I was young and she was still alive. An old song from her childhood.

After a day working in the fields, I was carefully washing the dust and sweat from my body in preparation for the coming night, as this day marked my passing into adulthood, and tonight there should be celebrations, and tomorrow I should come into my inheritance. This was the custom, because though my father still lived, I was the only son of an only child who was a female, and whose father, my grandfather, had owned the great farm that spread out for many leagues from the well in the courtyard where I bathed. His father, my great grandfather, had built the fortified farmhouse about the well and extended the lands his father had left him. But I doubted I would ever become master of the place, and I sang not from joy but to keep away the fear of what might happen to me that night, and to recall the good times when my mother and grandfather still lived.

"I am weary from the road," a stranger's deep voice said, startling me from my brooding, and I spun about.

A man, no, a giant, a god, was walking toward me. His golden hair curled about his face, his skin was golden, his body muscular and of a great size, but graceful as a cat. I was almost overwhelmed by the sight of him, for I confess that I greatly admire men of beauty. And he was truly magnificently beautiful.

Gathering my wits, I greeted him as our customs required me to. "Welcome stranger," I said, my eyes traveling

145

all over his magnificent body, his only clothing a pale leather loincloth and the belts that secured his weapons upon his back. "I am Hilaron, only son of Margaret, daughter of Mortho . . ." Then I hesitated, uncertain for a moment, before I continued with pride, ". . . who today will become master of this house. If you come in peace, you are welcome here," I said, as was the custom in our region, and I was suddenly gladdened to speak with pride of my lineage and inheritance to even one stranger on that special day.

"I am Konan, and yes, I come in peace," he replied, "and thank you for your welcome, Hilaron, son of Margaret, daughter of Mortho and master of this fine house." His response thrilled me, and I was aware of his eyes exploring my nakedness as plainly as mine had explored him. "I have traveled far and am weary of the road and seek a bed for the night."

"You are . . . welcome to a bed," I replied, gulping and unable not to think of him in my bed, though my eyes drifted from him to the open gates into the courtyard, knowing that my father would soon return and that he might not welcome a stranger in his house, on this night of all nights. Then I wondered if perhaps my father had sent for this man Konan. But no, I was sure my father was too mean with his gold, my gold now, if I lived through the night, to do such a thing.

"If you wish to wash the sweat and dust of your journey off you, I shall draw water from the well for you," I said to Konan, for now he was close, standing but an arm's length from me, I saw that he was dusty from the road and streaks of sweat ran down him.

He accepted my offer, and I was glad, if for no other reason than that my manhood was growing at the very closeness of him and washing him meant I could hide it from him. He was such a magnificent man, and his scent was strong, and I was embarrassed and still slightly uncertain if he was merely an innocent traveler passing by or not.

"I gladly accept your offer," he replied courteously, and with obvious pleasure he removed the fine sword, quiver of arrows, small lance, and his bow from his back and set them

146

aside, the leather straps that held them having left pale honey-colored damp strips across his golden skin where the sun had not reached it. Then I was almost unable to breath as he undid his loincloth and set it aside, and I confess I could not take my eyes from what it had only half hidden before.

Ahhh. He was as big there as anywhere, and his balls were full and large, and I was sure his weapon was partly firm it was so long and full and the head was peeping free of its pocket. He was the most magnificent man I had ever set my eyes on. A man such as young men dream of. A wild barbarian, but one more like the gods than ordinary men. That he should arrive on this day of all days made it seem as if the gods were smiling on me at last. For I had formed a plan for the coming night, but one not easy to carry out alone.

Konan stepped up beside me in the trough, and I quickly filled the bucket with cool, clear water from the well. He took it from my hands and poured the water over his head and let it run refreshingly down his chest and back. Then he gave the bucket back to me, and I filled it again, and as he stood with his back to me, I poured it over his back and shoulders myself.

We continued in that way for some time, me drawing up the water from the well and pouring it over him as he moved about and used his hands to rub the dust and sweat away. Then suddenly he turned, and smiling at me broadly, took the bucket from me as I began trembling, and poured it over me. My trembling was caused by what I now saw, for when he turned, I saw clearly his huge manhood was now standing up tall and solid, thick and long, its head full and dark, and the water was dripping from it as if it leaked its juice already. I melted for him then. And my breathing became unsteady.

My manhood also stood hard and firm now, a goodly size and even straighter then his and bouncing on my belly as I moved. And the cool water he poured over me could not reduce the heat and need I felt. We both were as clean as babes by now, and wet, and glittering in the sunlight. And I ached for

147

this magnificent giant, Konan, to take me. Yet I could not help glancing nervously at the gate.

"Who are you watching for?" Konan asked.

"Who? Um. My father and his . . . his stepson," I stammered haltingly.

Then, as he smiled at me with hooded eyes, Konan reached for my manhood and gripped it in his fist. I stood there, unable to pull away, though I did not wish the servants or my returning father to see us. But then, with a gasp, I cried, "No, not here," and pushed his hand off me. And I was looking about wildly for a place we might go to be private, for I wanted nothing more at that moment than to be taken by him. To feel . . . to feel possessed by his power and strength.

"Perhaps you have a stable to show me. Such a fine farm as this must have many fine beasts in its stable," he said in a quiet slow voice, smiling at me with lust-filled eyes, and I quivered at what I knew he was really saying. That we were like animals in heat with but one overwhelming desire.

"Yes," I stammered, "Yes, we have a fine stable. Over there," I added, pointing to the side of the courtyard by the entrance gate.

But instead of rushing there, Konan only stepped out of the trough and took up one of the sheets of linen I had set on a stool nearby and held it out in his spread arms.

"You are wet," he said, "and so am I. As your guest, I shall dry you as thanks for you washing the dust off me. Then you shall take me to your stable."

I stepped out of the trough and into the linen sheet he held open, and he worked it over me with his large, strong hands. Ahhhh. Those hands and that soft linen. He caressed my body with the fabric, and though I was already almost overcome by my lust for him, he still increased the fire raging in my blood.

"Yes," I gasped and moaned. "Let's go to the stable; I am ready," I begged him, pressing myself to him, taking hold of myself and stroking. But he ignored my pleas, and instead he wiped all about my manhood and caressed my body. Finally, he

148

wrapped the soft, fine towel about my balls and gently rubbed them dry. I was whimpering now, and if I were not a man, I might have wept with frustration. Then he turned me about, and I was having trouble standing as he ran the linen up my crease, rubbing it gently back and forth across the entrance to my passage.

Then as I stood there helplessly watching, he quickly ran the linen sheet over himself, finally stroking it gently along his great manliness as I watched. Then at last, he took up his sword and other weapons and his loincloth, and said, "The stable, Hilaron."

And I turned and led the way, almost running.

We entered the stable, and I moved along nervously, my manhood throbbing now and leaking its juices already, until I got to the stall where my old horse, Moran, was resting.

"This was my mother's horse, and before that her father's, and she loved him dearly. But now Moran is mine, though he is very old," I said and turned for Konan, leaning against the railings of the stall and looking in at Moran as Konan moved close behind me. I felt a wet finger sliding into my crease and rubbing over my entrance, which twitched at his slightest touch. Then Konan turned my head and kissed me deeply and his tongue battled mine; I moaned, and, reaching for my throbbing tool, I fisted it briefly and spouted my seed.

Then he broke the kiss, and I watched old Moran take a mouthful of hay as Konan pressed the tip of his wet finger into my hole before I cried out in surprise as he put his hands on my waist and lifted me up to set my feet on the middle rail. I gripped the top rail of the stall to steady myself, which left me slightly bent over.

And words nearly escape me, for then that great god of a man, Konan, had his fingers spreading my cheeks and exposing my entrance, and I widened my legs, wanting what he had for me and opening myself more.

But what he did was to bend his head and bring his mouth to my quivering hole, and his tongue teased at my puckered rim, wetting it well and making it twitch and open.

149

Then his great tongue, as big as many men's swords, dove into the opening and worked in and out of me. I moaned and almost lost my balance on the rail. But his hands gripped my hips strongly, keeping me from falling.

When Konan withdrew his tongue I felt a thick long finger at my ass. And he pressed it into my now well-wet and opened hole. I started to lose my grip on the rails again as that finger worked its way up inside my channel, and my hips fell back until my butt rested on his chest, and Konan reached his other hand around and took my engorged manhood in it and began to stroke me, as his finger pumped in and out of me. I came again; I was young, and I shot that load of cream across old Moran's back, before collapsing back even more, so that my butt slid down Konan's chest as I went weak and lost my grip on the rail.

Konan laughed as he caught me and pushed me back up, "Turn around and lock your arms over the rail," he said, and with some effort I did, now looking into his face, seeing his lust filled eyes and softly smiling mouth. And his eyes locked on mine as I came down, my arms stretched back to hold me up.

And as I looked into his dark eyes and felt as if I might drown in them, Konan lifted my feet and placed one on each of his shoulders and moved in close between my thighs, taking some of the weight off my upper arms.

I believe I was moaning then, for Moran nuzzled my arms as if worried about me. "Settle, settle, Moran," I murmured, as I looked down and saw Konan's hand moving beneath my package. His fingers began to work again at my hole as he smiled at me and then leant in and kissed me, deeply again. Oh such a deep possessing kiss, his body pressing my legs back and helping me stay upright. His tongue exploring my mouth and dancing with mine.

His other hand cupped my ass cheek as his fingers moved to open me, and soon I was hard again and throbbing and dribbling juice from the slit in the head of my manhood.

When he pulled his fingers out of me, he broke our kiss and I whimpered at the loss of the fullness. But then he was holding his hard club and rubbing the flaming head of it up the inside of my thighs, under my sac and along my own manhood. I was moaning loudly and arching at the feel of it before he even stroked the knob over the twitching entrance to my channel.

"Spear me; plunge your mighty weapon to my heart," I cried, my body trembling as I looked down at that huge organ and watched its cap disappear between my spread thighs and behind my sac. I felt it pressing at me, and, with a kick of his hips, Konan had forced it into me, and I let out a cry of pain. But I also watched, whimpering and fascinated, as the length of his shaft disappeared slowly—so slowly—up inside me. He allowed me to adjust. But even though he took his time, I still threw my head back and panted and whimpered, he went so deep. Then I looked down between my thighs at my again-hard weapon against my belly, and I could see no more of his shaft, just his golden haired bush making a nest for my balls, as I felt his hair brushing my ass.

I shook with wonder at having taken all of that great weapon in my channel. And then slowly he began to move it about in me. "Oh," I gasped, at the sudden pain. "No, oh, yes," I cried loudly as he moved in and out, but I continued to cry out and beg him to go on, and on. Konan finally began a fierce driving up into me, lifting me up bodily with each thrust, before he froze and shuddered, and I felt his seed explode inside me. And he threw his head back and roared as he filled me. The roar of some great beast celebrating his power and strength. I shook with exhaustion as he finally withdrew his mighty organ from my passage, and I felt liquid running out of my hole as he gently stepped backwards and lifted my feet down one by one and held my waist so I could drop to the floor gently and release my aching arms from the rail. Then he clasped his strong arms around me and gently held me to him, taking my mouth in another deep kiss as I wrapped my arms about his neck and shared the kiss while I regained my strength.

When I could finally stand unaided, I remembered my duty as a host. "You must be hungry and thirsty," I stammered. "I am a poor host. Come into the house and I will have food brought for you," I said, feeling Konan's man juice running down my thighs as I wrapped the damp linen sheet about my waist and led him out of the stable.

We had barely entered the courtyard when two men on horseback came through the gates and several servants suddenly appeared and rushed to meet them.

It was my father, David, and my stepbrother, Lucus, returning.

The Selfish Father

All was arranged, and it was with light hearts and in anticipation of the removal of the last annoying inconvenience that stopped me from fully enjoying the wealth of my property that we rode back home.

My son, Hilaron's, entry into his estate would be celebrated well that night with a small party. I had invited a few young men of the local area to attend and had planned on the night being one of special celebration for me, rather than Hilaron. And as we departed from Yarron's farm I laughed out loud at how well things had been arranged.

Lucus and I arrived at the ford, and before crossing the river, we stopped to water our horses and take a drink ourselves. My mood was so good that I pulled Lucus to me and kissed him as I gripped his phallus through his clothes and squeezed it hard. He shook and gasped but did not pull away. He liked it rough. I lifted my robe, and he fell to his knees and sucked on my engorging rod until it was rock hard, at which point I took the small thick handled whip from my belt, and Lucus briefly sucked on the hard handle of that, wetting it down. Then he lifted his robe and bent over, spreading his cheeks with his hands and showing me his ass.

After a few flicks of the whip across his pale ass cheeks, reddening them, I turned the whip around and the handle slid into his entrance with the ease of long practice. I enjoyed watching it pumping in and out of his hole as I beat my own hard rod against his ass and thighs and he moaned and whimpered and wriggled his butt so the stiff handle stroked new parts of his channel. When I tired of that, I removed the handle from him, hearing a nice slurping, and then replaced it with my own weapon and pumped him long and hard, while occasionally flicking the whip over his ass and thighs. I came inside him, most satisfied, and I think he finished himself off afterward as I heard a moaning noise as I tidied myself and went to drink more water from the clear, fast-flowing stream.

We continued our ride back to the farm even more satisfied, and I was sharing a joke about the coming night with my companion, Lucus, who is my step-son from my first wife and not much younger than myself, when we entered the courtyard of my large farm and the servants came running to help me from my horse.

But at that moment my day was spoiled. For as soon as we rode into the courtyard, I found myself facing an apparition, a shocking and perhaps dangerous one.

Hilaron, that unfortunate product of my union with his mother, Margaret, my last wife, was walking from the stable with a well-armed barbarian of huge size. And by Hilaron's look, they had been doing more than looking over the old horse he kept inside the stables, which was the only animal there at present.

"The young devil," I hissed under my breath, flicking my whip at Lucus, who was gawking open mouthed at the pair. "Stop looking like a fool," I added, for unfortunately Lucus was not always as quick as I could have wished.

"You have a guest," I said loudly to Hilaron, unable to conceal the disapproval in my voice.

"Konan is a traveler who has asked a bed for the night," Hilaron replied with that arrogance he was prone to at times.

"A weary traveler is usually not so well armed," I replied, unable to stop myself from saying it.

The huge barbarian himself said nothing, but Hilaron had to say, "He comes in peace and is our guest," his face flushing red.

I knew what was going on, but the man looked too big and dangerous to confront in the courtyard in broad daylight.

He was a truly magnificent giant, golden skinned, muscular, and from the look of the bulging of his loincloth, endowed like a giant there also. I had no doubt Hilaron had enjoyed his attentions in the stable, the arrogant, scheming young fool.

"If he is weary, then you had best have food prepared and a bed made up for him," I said, wanting this man, Konan, asleep or at least unarmed and resting, as soon as possible. We had guests arriving before sunset, and I wanted nothing to upset my plans for the night's celebration.

* * * *

"Did you see his sword? The one across his back?" Lucus said, "That is a Mogul prince's sword. How did a man like that get such a thing? He must be some bandit. He is probably wanted by the soldiers of the Great Mogul."

"Unfortunately, the Great Mogul's soldiers are not nearby, so that is of no use to us now, Lucus. But he is being well fed, and if Hilaron has pleased him already, let's just hope he takes my son to his bed with him right after he has eaten. If he rides young Hilaron again, that may tire him and may give us an opportunity to take him unawares and remove him."

"You mean we should kill him? When he is a guest?" Lucus asked, sounding shocked at the idea.

"I have no doubt Hilaron has hired this giant to ruin all our plans, so he can take over the farm and dispossess us, perhaps even kill us." I told Lucus.

"Oh. Do you really think that? Hilaron? I didn't think he had it in him to think of such a thing. The young devil." Lucus replied, chuckling.

Once my horse, and Lucus's Donkey, had been led away to the stable, we entered the house, but not by the door to the kitchens as Hilaron and Konan had. We entered through the main door and into the central family area as was appropriate for the master of the house. And master of that fine house and all its lands I was and master was what I intended to remain.

Hilaron's treachery in bringing the stranger among us had me suddenly nervous, though, for as Lucus had said, I had not thought of my son as being so devious. But then, Hilaron had always done the unexpected and inconvenient.

"From the day he was conceived in the marriage bed, Hilaron has been nothing but trouble," I said angrily, once Lucus and I were in private again.

"He should never have lived," he replied.

"No, he should not," I agreed.

Being good looking and intelligent, I had in my young days married Lucus's mother, an older widowed woman with no other family whom I had wed for her property. I had worn her out with my demands on her both in the marriage bed and out of it, and she had soon died. Then setting my sights higher, I had married a pale, thin woman, Margaret, the only surviving child of a very wealthy and lecherous father who had produced many children, mostly female, all of whom, apart from this one frail daughter, had died in infancy. I had every reason to be optimistic that any child my new wife managed to produce would be a girl and also that it was most unlikely to survive, and the birth could easily be the death of her. All good points in Margaret's favor in my view, because then on her father's death, all the property that was his would become mine.

It had seemed a most satisfactory match, and having bedded her roughly and repeatedly till she was sickly and obviously with child, I left to visit my own farm some distance away, where Lucus still lived. Margaret's father would not have Lucus live with me at my new home. The old man was a nuisance, and though half crippled, he refused to die. Margaret's care of him was too good, but there was little I could do about it, as the old man had several brothers and cousins still living around about, all of whom were land holders of some wealth.

I stayed away until I knew Margaret was approaching her time and had good hopes that when I returned, I would be weeping to find my wife on the point of death, if not dead already, and the child gone with her. And I knew her father would depart this life soon after.

But, no. Instead of returning to play the grieving husband, I found my wife, Margaret, delivered early of a small son, and her father revitalized by the birth. This had seemed a minor setback, as the child was small and there was that history of dead infants behind her. But then my wife wailed and wept so much when I took my marital rights with her that I turned to taking the servant girls instead, and then I argued with my father-in-law over some minor point of discipline that involved me beating the servant he was then having in his bed, and I gladly returned to my farm and my far more obliging step-son, Lucus.

I could wait a few months till our weak-looking son died.

Unfortunately, the boy child, Hilaron, did not die in infancy, and as I moved back and forth between my two homes, I found that each time I arrived at my wife's farm the boy had grown bigger and stronger. But still I had plans for the day my father-in-law finally had the decency to leave us.

"Do you think they have finished eating yet?" Lucus asked eagerly.

"Uh?" I was dragged back from my brooding on how badly things had turned out. "They should have, and I am sure the giant can think of better things to do to fill his time than sitting about eating. We shall go to the kitchens and see what is going on," I replied.

But the barbarian was still eating, and by the pile of bones, skins and remains before him he had already eaten enough for half a dozen normal men.

"Wine," I cried, "why is there no wine for my guest? Bring it now," I ordered, for there was none on the table at which the monster and Hilaron sat. There was only what looked like a jug of goat's milk such as children might drink. Hilaron had taken much of it when young. Wine was a far more suitable drink in the circumstances. "The best," I yelled to the running servant.

The better the wine was, the more this Konan would drink, I was sure. These barbarian swords for hire I knew would drink all they could get their hands on.

"And where do you travel from, Konan?" I asked from politeness.

"From the West," he replied, before falling on another plate of fine meats.

"I have also been to the West," I replied proudly, "but I have been all the way to the magnificent palace of the Great Mogul himself. To pledge the loyalty of this region," I boasted, "I have seen its wonders and been admitted to the great hall where the mogul sat upon his throne. I saw him from some distance, true, but few men get closer to him than I."

"It is a wondrous place," Konan replied and said no more.

He was a rough and stupid man who could do nothing but eat and drink and take his carnal pleasures whenever he wanted, I was sure. And who would soon be drunk on my wine, and no more trouble.

"Hilaron, be sure to show this . . . traveler to his bed and give him more wine and whatever else he needs to make him comfortable."

"As you command, Father," Hilaron said, looking at me with his calculating eyes.

I hated him. The only way my son could serve me was dead.

Lucus and I returned to the central area of the house, and I saw he was stroking his organ and his eyes were glazed. "On your knees," I ordered him.

It was obvious that the barbarian visitor, Konan, was hung like a donkey and Lucus was aroused by what he had seen of his manhood as it tented his loincloth. And if Lucus wanted to be serving anyone, it was going to be me. He knelt obligingly and, gripping my quickly hardening manhood, he sighed, "Oh the barbarian truly is a magnificent animal," and fed my growing rod to his lips, his experienced mouth muscles gripping me firmly but gently as he slid his head down. I sank deep into the opening and teased at his throat. Soon I heard him moan, and his mouth stopped its perfect sucking as he came. I pulled free of his lips, and he almost toppled over as he spurted another shot of his juice across the floor.

"Over the bed. Quickly," I growled at him, holding my throbbing weapon and stroking it.

Lucus stumbled to his feet, and lifting his loose robe up, he fell across the bed. I was between his thighs and plowing him deep and hard in no time at all. And as I rode him, I imagined that great barbarian interloper riding young Hilaron to death, splitting him with his huge, engorged barbarian weapon, and with those good thoughts in my head, I filled Lucus's belly with more cream than I had spouted for a long time.

The Wicked Guests

"Do you have your knife?" Goron asked his brother, Joseph.

The brothers were both good looking young men, bronzed by the sun from time spent working in their fertile fields and grown tall and muscular on their land's produce. But they were ambitious also. And eager for wealth, and to show their strength. And on this special day, the two young men had oiled and combed their hair, dressed in their best linen tunics, and were mounted on their donkeys for the short journey that lay ahead. And now that they were leaving the farmyard of their family's home, they could talk freely, being out of earshot of their father and his workers.

"Of course. You think I am a fool? Ha. Though we will not need a knife to deal with young Hilaron," Joseph replied, "It's a good plan that his father, David, has formed."

"Yes. It is. We are going to have a good night, brother—food, wine, blood, and gold," Goron replied, as he laughed aloud. "A very good night. But I won't trust David until the gold is in our hands."

"I don't trust him either. Perhaps we should see the gold before, rather than after, the deed is done. So, do you also have your knife, brother?" Joseph asked.

Goron pulled a long, dangerous blade, which could almost have been called a short sword it was so large, from the belt at his waist and held it up to the sun so it glittered evilly. "See, the sun god knows it shines with eagerness for Hilaron's father's blood if he tries to cheat us," he replied, joining in his brother's laughter.

They rode on a short distance to another stone farmhouse, much like the one they had left, though slightly larger. But not as large as the house where Hilaron and his father, David, and step-brother, Lucus, lived. But like the brother's, Goron and Joseph's, own home, it was still the dwelling of a wealthy farmer and his family.

A servant waited at the gates of the house for the brothers' arrival and took the reigns of their donkeys from them as they dismounted. "Welcome," he said, "Your cousins have been told of your arrival." And as he spoke they saw three young men emerging to welcome them, all dressed in their finest linen robes.

"Yarron, Matthew, and Zanar, we come in peace," Goron cried out in greeting to them, as was the custom.

"And good you do," Zanar joked. "There are three of us, and we can take you two scrawny fools on any day, and win. So I bid you welcome, cousins."

"What? Scrawny!" Goron cried, leaping forward and waving his long knife under his cousin's nose.

"Save it for tonight," Yarron hissed. "Save it for Hilaron and David, and perhaps Lucus, the soft woman that he is."

"Or better still, old Peter. Perhaps we will take his ripe daughter off his hands on our way home," Zanar added, laughing.

"Ah. A poor orphan girl needs protection," Matthew cried out in mock distress, as the five young men joined together in laughter.

"Old Peter's daughter is ripe, true enough, and her father is no real obstacle, dead or alive," Goron added thoughtfully, obviously taken by the idea.

"Lets earn our gold first by celebrating Hilaron's coming of age," Zanar counseled, and the whole group became serious for a moment.

"There should be little trouble there," Goron said, and everyone nodded their heads happily in agreement.

"We agree on that," Yarron said, "so come inside, and we'll start the celebrations, then depart in good spirits," he added, inviting them into the stone hall of the house.

Two manservants immediately came running to them with jugs of wine. They poured it out into a fine silver goblet for Yarron and fine clay ones for his brothers and guests, and then offered the men the goblets of wine and laid out platters of the finest food on the long table between the couches set up in the main hall. "Eat and drink. All of you," Yarron ordered them. "You are my guests." For though Yarron's father lived, he was unable to leave his bed, and the duties of head of the house had fallen on Yarron's young shoulders several years before. "I will tell you that I wonder at David ever giving this party for his son Hilaron. I had thought Hilaron would not live to see this day. He will not live to see another, true, but still it has surprised me."

"If Hilaron had not been at his great uncle Matthias's house when his grandfather died and had not been escorted home by him, with warnings made, I have no doubt he would not have lived this long," Joseph replied.

"Ah, but now fortunately he has upset old Matthias by being caught wandering into the stable with some young man, instead of asking for his granddaughter's hand," Yarron said and then clapped his hands together loudly, "And talking of young men, I have a new entertainment. One I am sure you will enjoy."

A young male servant of no more than nineteen years, and lean and lightly muscled and golden skinned, dressed only in the shortest and whitest of tunics appeared, carrying a jug of wine, and the other two servants quietly withdrew to the end of the room, ready if needed.

"This, cousins, is Salus," Yarron told them, indicating the handsome young man who had just entered and was walking toward him smiling. "And he is very entertaining."

Yarron's brothers murmured agreement as they reclined on their couches, and Yarron grabbed at the short robe Salus wore and pulled the young man to him. The youth

162

appeared to struggle and opened his dark eyes wide in fear, but as he didn't even spill a drop of wine, it appeared he didn't struggle very seriously, though a wary look remained in his eyes.

"Greet my guests, Salus," Yarron growled, one of his hands running up under the man's short tunic.

"Yes master," the young man said. "I welcome you all to my master's house. My only wish is to serve you and make your stay here more enjoyable."

"And greet my brothers also," Yarron added.

"As you say, master," Salus replied, smiling in an enticing way at the group of men reclining on their couches about him. "I greet your brothers," he said.

The men had grown quiet, some having some idea what came next and the others curious to discover what new entertainment awaited them.

"Well, Salus, you may serve us all before we leave for this party we are going to attend this evening."

Salus's eyes opened wide, and he looked worried for a moment. "Serve all those here, master?" he asked, "All . . . five of you big, strong young men?"

It was obvious to all that Yarron's hand had been stroking Salus's manhood beneath his tunic as it now tented the fabric in a most impressive manner and Yarron's other hand was stroking his own weapon, which was also showing it could reach a good size. "Yes. All five of us," Yarron hissed, stripping the linen tunic off Salus, to reveal his lean muscular body, and his hard, erect weapon, which was indeed of a very good size. "Though I think that most of the entertainment will have to wait till we return and have more time to celebrate."

Salus then bent his head downwards, and his hands lifted Yarron's robe to reveal his own hard, erect weapon, which was of an even larger and more impressive length and thickness. The others watched as Salus grasped it and fed it to his lips, while bending over in such a way that all could see his meaty ass cheeks and the crease between them. Yarron reached to Salus's ass and pulled it closer to him as he lay on his couch and the young man sucked and bobbed his head between his thighs.

"This is Salus's greatest asset," Yarron told his companions, as he parted Salus's cheeks and exposed his hole. "He uses it well, and often, and is greatly rewarded for the great pleasure it brings those lucky enough to enjoy it." Yarron dabbed a finger in some oil that was in a bowl on the table and then pressed it to Salus's hole, which opened out easily, so his finger slid right in. "See, well used," Yarron said, "and you shall all have full enjoyment of this treasure when we return. But, my cousins, let me see you take him now, while he feeds on me."

Goron and Joseph already had their robes lifted and were wide eyed and open mouthed, panting and fisting their own rods to hardness as they lay back on their couches. They were lying opposite Yarron and his brothers and enjoying the spectacle Yarron was providing them. At Yarron's order, they eagerly rose up and stepped up behind Salus, jockeying for the first turn at filling his channel with their throbbing organs. Yarron looked on eagerly, also panting, open mouthed and glazed eyed, as not more than a foot before him, Joseph and Goron both added at least one finger to the hole Yarron's still occupied. Salus wriggled his ass and widened his stance, preparing for the fun to come, the fingers digging and rotating inside him, forcing small gasps and moans to escape his busy mouth.

Yarron liked nothing better than to watch a man being plowed by others as he enjoyed him himself, and he withdrew his finger and reached for Salus's own bouncing manhood and his balls and played with them, but cruelly, as Goron pushed Joseph aside, and with one hand holding Salus's cheeks spread, he guided the head of his manhood to the young man's entrance with his other hand. And then he pushed. His organ was almost a hand's length long, but not thick, and it glided easily into Salus's well-oiled channel. He bottomed quickly, grinding his hips against the young man's ass.

"Now. Plow him! Hard and fast!" Yarron gasped, his hand pumping Salus's cock wildly as he moaned at what the young man's mouth was doing to his own weapon. And before his eyes Goron began to pound Salus's ass in deep, long strokes.

Goron came quickly, and Salus spouted his cream out at the same time, but Yarron held himself back. Goron slid out, and some of his cum dribbled out with him. Yarron eagerly reached a hand out and caught it and used it to lubricate his renewed painful squeezing of Salus's balls and softening manhood.

Joseph's weapon was thicker than his brother's and almost as long, so that when it entered him, Salus choked and grunted about Yarron's organ as he sucked and slid it in and out between his lips, and deep into his throat.

Meanwhile Yarron's own brothers, Matthew and Zanar, sat side by side upon a couch with a hand wrapped around each other's engorged rods, as their other hand roamed their chests, pinching their nipples and stroking their bellies, looking on with lust-filled eyes at their cousins taking of Salus, whom they had both ridden frequently already, though he had only been in the house for a moon and a half.

Joseph plowed him longer, but just as hard as his brother had, and Salus was moaning and his tool had reengorged and he came again as Joseph came inside him. When Joseph pulled out, his man juice ran from Salus's hole and down his thighs, and Yarron finally came, after rubbing his hand in it. As he did so, he shot his own seed into the sucking mouth of his young servant and moaned loudly.

For a short time after the five young men sat about and recovered, drinking and eating and talking listlessly. Meanwhile, Salus served them, still naked, and they occasionally fondled him or pulled him into their laps and played their hands over his chest and belly as well as his organ and his big, low-hanging balls.

But finally it was time to depart, for they needed to reach Hilaron's house before dusk, and Yarron sent Salus off. "Be ready to satisfy us all when we return," he said, leaning in as if to kiss him, but then biting Salus on the neck—where several bruises were visible—and laughing. There were bruises also on his flanks and ass. Salus winced at the pain of the bite, and his mouth, but not his eyes, smiled at his master and his companions as they left.

The five had their donkeys saddled and brought from the small stable, and mounting up, they took the road to the house of Hilaron, his father David, and step-brother Lucus.

And as soon as he could, Salus ran from the hall and along the passageway to the kitchens.

The Satisfied Barbarian

My first sight of young Hilaron bathing so openly and lit by the late-afternoon sun, making the water flowing over him sparkle and glitter as if he were radiating light like a young god, had overwhelmed me with desire for him. And as I entered the courtyard of that fine estate, I could not have stopped myself from having him if I had wanted to. Perhaps the gods truly had decided it should be that way. Or perhaps after my time in the Great Mogul's prison, I was just more than ready to enjoy a fine young man who looked at me with eyes equally full of surprise, admiration, and youthful lust.

And I greatly enjoyed burying my weapon deep inside his channel when I took him in the stables. Yes, after so many months of men presuming to have some right to me, I rejoiced in my freedom to once again take any man who caused the fires of desire to ignite in me. And the sight of young Hilaron bathing naked in the courtyard had certainly ignited those fires. He had easily made my weapon hard and aching, and as we left the stables, I had barely begun to satisfy my desire for him.

But I quickly discovered that I had chosen to enter a wealthy house where all was not as it seemed. Ah, all I wanted to do was enjoy young Hilaron, to the limit of our pleasure. And he had claimed he was also the master of the house I was now visiting, which was ideal, but as soon as we left the stable, I discovered the real situation was not so clear.

Two grown men of early middle years rode into the courtyard as young Hilaron and I emerged from the barn. Both were well built and good looking in the dark-haired and olive-skinned way of that area, and both sat their mounts well, so that I admired them both as they came toward us. One was riding on a fine small horse, a sign of great wealth in that region, and the other upon a donkey, as was normal for a well-to-do man there. But the fine-looking man upon the horse was obviously angry at seeing me there, and as the servants who had ignored my arrival earlier now came running from the house to meet the two riders, I knew that in spite of what Hilaron had told me, this rider was more the master in that house than my young lover was. If I had not been still mellow from the good taking I had just enjoyed, I might have left the house then, at the sight of them. But I did not leave, and perhaps the gods truly had decided to set me on a course I would have had no desire to take if I had been given a choice.

But the gods give us pleasures and take them away again without caring. As they give all men youth, and then old age.

"You have a guest," the man on horseback said, but it was no question, and he was unable to conceal the anger in his voice.

Young Hilaron stepped forward and replied, "Konan is a traveler who has asked for a bed for the night," speaking respectfully as a man should to his elders, though equals, and not as the master of that house would.

"A weary traveler is usually not so well armed, son Hilaron," the man replied, his eyes now full of venom and moving from me to my sword, which from force of habit I had already slung across my back, ready for use.

I was surprised that this was the young Hilaron's father and had seen few men so arrogant and openly hostile and wondered what reason he had to act that way unless it was that he knew and disapproved of the lusty activity his son and I had so recently enjoyed in his barn.

But then I looked at the other man, who hung back but whose eyes seemed to be devouring me, raking my body from head to foot with lust, his lips parted and his tongue wetting them. This man wanted to be taken by me, I knew. And I realized he might be Hilaron's stepbrother. I was surprised at

168

his age, for to me he looked of an age with the father. And from the way he was looking at me, the stepson was well used to sharing himself with other men, and I doubted it could be a secret from the father.

Young Hilaron spoke again, saying, "He comes in peace and is our guest," his face flushing red and a touch of anger in his voice. A voice that was firm now and manly, not the impassioned crying out or whispering voice I had heard earlier as I made love to him in the barn.

The father said nothing for a moment, only looking at me shrewdly as if weighing me up before he seemed to relax and replied angrily, "If this visitor is weary, then you had best have food prepared and a bed made up for him. Now take him inside."

And with that he turned away and dismounted, handing his reigns to a servant, who bowed low and mumbled, obviously afraid of the father's anger.

As Hilaron led me away and into the kitchens, I wondered why the gods had sent me to that one house to request a bed, instead of some other more peaceful house. And I noted how the stepbrother's eyes still followed me. And I wondered idly if he were as good a man to take as Hilaron. That young man may have assuaged my worst hunger for man flesh, but the atmosphere of the place I was in was far from conducive to rest and relaxation and the enjoyment of simple pleasure.

I had no fear for myself, though, and I was also amused by the petty ways of men. Then once we were seated in a small room near the kitchens and the elderly female cook and a servant had piled food upon the table, I discovered that the larder of the house was very well stocked, indeed, and eating became my primary concern. The men certainly did not go without in that regard, and I was more than ready to eat well and often for a few days.

"I apologize for my . . . father," Hilaron said shyly as we sat down. "He is . . . not an easy man."

"Hungh," the busy old cook snorted, then moved over to us and bent to whisper angrily, " If this great barbarian is a friend of yours, he will convince you to leave this house before tonight. For I doubt even he could protect you."

"Shhh," Hilaron hissed back at her. "I know he plans something, Miriam. I am prepared for it. After tonight this house is mine, and I will not walk away from my legacy of my grandfather. I am rightfully the master here after I spend a night in this house now I am of age. It's what tradition demands," he said to her and paused as if thinking. "Then I shall go to my great uncle Matthias and will have him and my cousins come and help me to remove my. . . father from here. And forbid him to ever return."

Miriam waved her hands helplessly. "You do not know how evil your father is," she hissed. "And you, you great strong barbarian, what are you here for then? Are you for Hilaron, or are you secretly here to serve his father, David?" she asked me angrily, her face flushed and her old body shaking. "Has he paid you to remove the last one who stops him owning all this?" she added, waving her arms again to indicate the stone walls about us.

"No, Miriam," Hilaron hissed, then looked at me fearfully for a moment. "You are not, are you? Are you here for my father? Answer me honestly," he begged me.

"No," I replied. "I am merely a weary traveler, and you saw that your father had no liking for me."

"All this he married my beloved Margaret to steal," Miriam continued. "Already he negotiates with lord Ananel, for his eldest daughter and a big dowry, as if you were already gone. He seeks to become a wealthy prince by his evil ways."

"Miriam, quiet," Hilaron hissed, now obviously deeply concerned at what she was saying as the other servant was moving about. "They will hear you. And Konan is a guest; this is none of his concern. It is only chance that he is here today."

"Chance? Hungh. And what of the gods? I have prayed and made sacrifices, begging they would help to stop David, or make you save yourself," she hissed, obviously also afraid of being overheard. "So maybe this barbarian has been sent to answer my prayers, may it be so. May it be so," she added, tears now on her cheeks as she turned back into the kitchen to baste a carcass roasting on a spit over the fire.

Ahh, what a den of intrigue and suspicion I had innocently walked into, and I wondered which of the gods was taking their amusement from my predicament, and that of young Hilaron, and all who dwelt in that house. For I was obviously a part of whatever was happening here, my very presence having created yet more layers of fear and uncertainty among its inhabitants.

"I thank you for a fine meal, Miriam, and will tell you no more than that so far no man has had enough gold to buy my sword to slay an innocent man in his own home. Though I have slain more than a few innocent men in battle, when that is the way of things," I said, loudly enough for her to hear.

Then Hilaron's father and his stepson were entering the kitchen, the father obviously angry and holding his temper with difficulty. He looked at the table where the remains of my meal so far were sitting on platters, seeing the bones and skin and unwanted pieces, then he shouted, "Wine," and asked, "Why is there no wine for my guest?" ordering, "Bring it now."

I was in fact drinking fresh goat's milk and good clean water, which was all I wanted. "The best," he yelled after the running servant, before turning and glaring at me again.

"And where do you travel from, Konan?" he asked.

"From the west," was all I replied. And I continued eating.

"I have been to the west," he replied proudly, "To the mighty palace of the Great Mogul himself. To pledge the loyalty of this region," he boasted. "I have seen its wonders and been admitted to the great hall where the mogul sat upon his throne. Few men get closer than I."

"It is a wondrous place," I replied politely as a guest should in a stranger's house, doubting Hilaron's father, David, had seen much of it as closely as I had.

"Hilaron, be sure to show this . . . this traveler to his bed soon, so he may rest, as we have a celebration tonight that I invite him to join. And give him more wine and whatever he needs to make him comfortable," he ordered, seeming to be even angrier now that he had seen me eating well.

"As you command, father," Hilaron replied politely.

And I was more than agreeable to being shown to a comfortable bed and made more comfortable there by Hilaron.

While the father talked, the stepson had again stood back, but I noted that his hand was stroking what appeared to be a good-sized and growing organ through the fabric of the light tunic he now wore. And I noted how it moved beneath the fabric as if it grew longer and thicker. But as I returned my eyes to the father, I noted that he too seemed to bulge beneath his clothing. And I became curious as to the situation between them.

And of course my curiosity, and the proximity of so many fine looking men, had my own weapon stirring.

"Drink, Konan, our wine is the finest," the father commanded me as the servant hurried back with a pitcher of wine.

Then the two men turned and left the room, and I reached beneath the table to Hilaron's lap and grasped what rested there under his light robe and between his parted thighs. He jumped and gave a small cry, "Come. Show me my bed," I ordered him.

Soon after I had Hilaron lying back on a comfortable bed and was again buried inside his fine ass and moving my weapon about so as to feel the pleasure of the different sensations his channel had to offer me, when I heard a noise by the door. I had deliberately left it partly open before I lay Hilaron back upon the fine bedding and took him again. Now as I continued to plow his fine ass, I looked about and smiled at the watching figure only partly seen beyond the frame.

"Come, join us," I said loudly enough for the watcher to hear, "Come, do not be afraid. I am in the mood to take any well-made man, as it's many months since I have freely taken any who pleased me and were willing."

Nothing happened, and I deliberately made deep long strokes into the ass of a writhing and loudly moaning Hilaron to show the full length and thickness of my weapon to the watcher. And I caressed Hilaron's own manhood, stopping the protest I had seen him thinking of making at hearing my invitation to the intruder.

"Come. Don't be afraid," I said firmly, ordering the spy to enter.

The spy emerged and showed himself to be the stepson, Lucus, as I had suspected. He entered the room cautiously, his eyes hooded with lust and fixed on where my pole moved in and out of Hilaron's hole. Meanwhile, the stepson's hand jerked up and down his own good-sized rigid length, which was now pulled free of his tunic.

"Come," I said again, and he approached more closely, but still hesitantly.

But finally he had come close enough that I could reach out and clasp the head of his manhood and feel the juice leaking from it, and I did just that.

"That is a fine tool you have, but I think it is your hole I would rather see," I said pulling him to me and taking his mouth roughly as I continued to pump Hilaron.

"I am Lucus," he said, as I broke the kiss, and his voice was shaking with desire. But he looked at Hilaron nervously in spite of his lust, almost as if afraid of him, though Hilaron was arching his back and grasping at the sheets and moaning loudly, close to letting his own seed shoot free.

"Bend over," I ordered Lucus, and he quickly obliged and presented his ass to me, parting his cheeks and showing me a well-used hole that seemed lubricated already. I plunged a finger into it, pushing it deep and rotating it as he grunted. Then I pushed and pulled it back and forth while I leant my head back and roared as I filled Hilaron's quivering passage with my seed. Hilaron cried out also, and I looked down to see his own release shoot up his body as I gave him yet another load.

But then it was Lucus's turn, for he was almost as desirable as Hilaron. So as he eagerly bent over and licked the cream from Hilaron's body, I took my still-firm weapon and pressed it into his well-opened and lubricated entrance and began a slow fucking of him. Soon Lucus had cleaned Hilaron's belly up and his head moved down to the young man's manhood, where he continued his licking by following the veins down it to its head, which he took into his mouth, sucking on it before moving on to taking Hiaron's big balls between his lips and gently mouthing them both at once.

I hummed with pleasure at the sight and enjoyed the even greater pleasure of an experienced channel quivering about my buried weapon as I made my explorations of Lucus's ass.

Young Hilaron could not resist later when Lucus began to lick his ass and lubricate and open it again, and I pulled my rod free of Lucus's hole and plunged it again into Hilaron's for a short plowing before returning to Lucus's ass and using my fingers in Hilaron. And going back and forth between them in that pleasant way I filled some considerable time, until I finally threw my head back and roared again as my body shook and my cream shot deep inside Lucus. So making both men mine.

Lucus stood up shaking, and I kissed him on the mouth, "You have a fine ass," I said, and I grasped his throbbing manhood, "and a fine tool," I added as he stood quivering.

I looked at Hilaron, who lay spread eagled upon the bed as I stroked Lucus pole. "What I have in my hand will please you greatly, Hilaron," I said and I lifted one of his legs and guided Lucus's manhood to that young man's entrance before he could object. Lucus fucked Hilaron in a wild frenzy and came quickly as Hilaron complained and objected.

"No," I said, "Do not complain. You should not be enemies. And now you shall fuck Lucus."

Lucus collapsed onto the bed as Hilaron jumped up and quickly drove his long fine tool viciously into Lucus's ass, aiming to hurt him, but unable too, before he plowed him hard and deep. Meanwhile, I tied Lucus's hands to the bed frame, and he had hardly realized this until after Hilaron pulled out and came over his back.

"Now," I said, "Lucus, you will tell us what Hilaron has to fear from his father, David, tonight."

In a wild panic Lucus struggled against the bonds holding him, and when he looked at me, his eyes were rolling in terror. I saw that fear would not make him talk, so I untied him and ran my hands over his body soothingly but held him firm as he struggled again to escape.

"Now, tell me, for I see you are as afraid of your father as . . ."

"He is not my father," Lucus cried angrily, "My father was a fine man who died an honest death. David has stolen my inheritance just as he plans to steal Hilaron's."

I looked at Hilaron, "So, it is true," I said, and Hilaron grunted and sat down beside us. "Why do you stay by him then, if you don't like him?" he asked Lucus angrily. "Apart from the fact he fucks you well."

"For many reasons," Lucus murmured, and stopped struggling. "Yes, he fucks well and often, but is also rough and thinks only of his own needs. But in the beginning I gave him what he wanted, because I hoped he'd leave me at my mother's farm and I'd live in peace there, as its overseer, if not its owner. But . . . but that was not to be. Your grandfather made that impossible."

"And when he first returned after marrying your mother, Margaret, I thought it was not for long, so I lay with him again, as he wanted me to. And . . . and it is easier to do that than to try to make a life for myself now, for I am a man with nothing but the clothes he stands up in who is used to living better than a beggar."

"So tell us of David's plans for tonight," I said, holding Lucus's shoulders and fixing his eyes with mine.

The Lucky Servants

The cook scurried along the passage trying to look invisible, which wasn't easy for a man of his height and solidness. And in one hand he held a sack that looked well filled but from the way it bounced about was not heavy. He made it to the kitchen unobserved, and entering, placed the sack in a corner out of sight, while looking sternly at the thin young woman, little more than a girl, who sat at the wooden trestle table grinding walnuts in a stone bowl

"You may go, Gila," he said to the young woman, who looked at him in wide-eyed surprise.

"Oh," she said uncertainly, "But . . ."

"Gila. Go," he said firmly, his brows furrowing in a way that indicated he was annoyed.

She hesitated still, but then muttered, "Thank you, Mark. Oh, thank you," and scurried out, eager to get out of sight, before her usually demanding master changed his mind.

Mark was the cook, but also a winemaker and herbalist, a man with many skills and of much importance in that house and in the ancient world.

"Humph," Mark mumbled. "If he doesn't come with me I am going anyway," he said to the empty room as he reached under the table Gila had been sitting at.

He pulled out a large wicker basket on leather straps that hooked over a man's shoulders, letting him carry the basket on his back. And lifting the cover off it and pulling a small square of linen out he poured the half crushed walnuts from the stone bowl into it and folded the cloth up, making a neat parcel.

"Yarron will hate to know I have taken food from his house, almost as much as he will hate me if I take Salus from him," the cook mumbled, as he placed the small parcel of nuts securely among the basket's contents.

As Mark was pushing the basket back out of sight, a young male servant entered the room carrying an empty jug. "Yarron has moved on to some entertainment with your young friend, whom he plans on sharing about generously when they return from this celebration at David's house," the servant said, as he set the jug on a high shelf.

"How many of them are there?" the cook asked worriedly.

"Five, of course, Goron and his brother, Joseph, and our three young men. They are also talking of Old Peter's daughter," the young man replied before he hesitated and blushed, "Talking of . . . of making some fun with her on their way back, and . . . I may . . . if I can get out of course. Can I go and warn her? Her father, . . . he, well you know he is a drunk; he will be no protection for her."

"Go. Go," the cook said, " Do what you can, but be here in the morning at first light. I doubt they will return before then, but if you are not here, you know what can happen."

"Well, I do, Mark," the servant replied, and spat into the smoldering fire. "Though I will not have to suffer as young Barabus did," he said. " But there are worse masters than Yarron, as well as better."

"True," the cook replied. But when the young servant had gone, he added, "But not many are worse by my reckoning, certainly not for poor Barabus."

Shortly afterward another servant hurried in, this one older, with his eyes slitted and his mouth slack. He was carrying another jug and several empty platters, which he hurriedly dumped on a high shelf, "There will be some fun tonight," he muttered, avoiding the cooks eyes and hurrying off, his hand gripping his hard pole through his short tunic even as he left the room. He was obviously hard and throbbing and in need of release.

"May the gods give Yarron the wasting sickness," the cook, Mark, cursed as he paced about the kitchen anxiously.

He muttered and looked at the doorway and occasionally went out into the passageway and listened, but each time he returned to the kitchen to continue his pacing and occasional mutterings.

Then Salus was suddenly coming through the doorway looking pale. "I believe all you have said about what befell poor Barabus," he said to Mark. "Yarron would have them all use me, when they return. Roughly, I have no doubt. I am afraid of what might happen to me, afraid that the injuries Barabus suffered . . ."

"You will leave with me then?" Mark interrupted with a cry, fear and excitement battling on his face and changing his whole appearance, as he moved to the young man and embraced him, his mouth finding Salus's, and the two falling into a deep kiss.

When their lips parted Salus's eyes were full of relief also, and he spoke rapidly. "Yes. Yes. I do not want to be ruined, to suffer . . . or to . . . to die of Yarron's abuse. I believe the stories now, about Barabus. Can we leave here? Now, Mark? You said . . . Please. Now."

"Yes. Yes. I have everything ready. Your possessions, mine—and some gold. I have even organized for us to ride some way on the smith's cart."

A greatly relieved Salus wrapped his arms more tightly about Mark, and they kissed again as Salus rubbed his body against the big, strong frame of the cook. Mark, in turn, was now quivering with desire at the closeness of the young man he was enamoured of and was so tightly embracing.

"Come. Come. Hurry," Mark said, flushed and shaking, but pulling away from Salus enough to drag his basket from beneath the table, as well as a cloth bundle, but not letting go of his lover—as if afraid the young man might suddenly change his mind and disappear. "I have family still in Persepolis, and there is work always for a man of my skills."

"Persepolis? Oh. Such a great city. We are going there?" Salus replied, in awe.

"Yes, to Persepolis," Mark replied, "Your things," he added, pointing to the sack in the corner of the room, which Salus grabbed up and briefly looked into.

"Thank you," Salus was saying as he turned back to Mark and saw the look on his face and smiled. "Do we have time . . . ?"

Mark hesitated, but then putting down his baggage, he moved to Salus and ran his hands down the younger man's back to the firm mounds of his rear and pulled his lover close to him, pressing his body to Salus's, as they fell into another deep, passionate kiss.

For long moments they melded into one being, and the world about them, with all its problems, vanished. Salus was hard and aching to be enclosed by warm flesh and rubbed his throbbing organ against Mark's firm, warm thigh as the big, strong hands at his ass lifted his short tunic and spread his cheeks.

"Hmmmmmmmmm," Mark rumbled, overcome by desire. And pulling his mouth free, he turned Salus about and pushed him down over the table. "Ah, so perfect," he sighed, as his hands again parted Salus's cheeks and he saw his hole. It was slick with cum still, inviting and quivering in anticipation, and Mark quickly lifted his robe, and taking his manhood in his hand, he stroked his cap slowly over the wet entrance, moaning as he did so, desperate for them to be joined. Then he was moving it about the puckered and twitching entrance to Salus's channel before he pressed himself in. There was some resistance, for he was thicker than any of the young men earlier had been, as well as longer.

Salus moaned, wanting the ultimate joining as much as his lover. "Oh gods," he cried out, and moved about to open himself more, feeling pain for a moment as the thick organ was pressed against the resistance his body made to such a huge thing trying to enter it. And then it was past. And after a sharp cry at the pain, it was as always only the waves of pleasure that Mark's big weapon always brought him as it moved into his body and rubbed against his spot.

Mark kissed the back of Salus's shoulders and neck as he moved inside him, and Salus mumbled happily, "Oh, that feels so good. Oh yes, deeper. All of you, I want all of you, Oh, Oh. Yesss."

And as Mark plowed him, Salus began to pump his hips back and forth to meet the big mans thrusts.

The excitement and the danger worked with his arousal, and Mark was soon moaning and taking his last thrust and coming deep inside his lover. Then he fell across his back and his arm circled under the young man and stroked him to his own quick release as he nuzzled at his neck.

"Ahh, I am a lucky man," Mark hummed in Salus's ear as the young man shuddered and the cream spouted from his weapon.

For a while they continued to lie like that, savoring the mellow afterglow of a deep joining, and Salus turned his face so their mouths met and they kissed again. Finally, Mark rose up and pulled his lover gently up and tidied his tunic. "Come, it's time to go."

Salus mumbled contentedly, smiling foolishly at the big man, as they both took up their possessions.

Putting his arm about Salus, Mark guided him to the door, "Now, we leave this cursed place," Mark said, and he spat into the smoldering fire.

Salus did the same, and then they were both hurrying toward the door that led to the outside world beyond the courtyard of the farm. But even as they made their departure, Mark kept his arm gently about Salus's shoulders as if still afraid he might vanish.

The Cunning Barbarian

There had been a great display of food and wine all evening, and the servants were constantly moving about, filling our cups again and offering us rich treats.

Present were Hilaron's family—his father; his stepbrother; his uncle, Matthias; and his two sons—and also five local men not much older than Hilaron, whom David had invited. They were cousins and were all fine-looking young men and sat and lay on three couches set along one side of the hall. David, Hilaron's father, reclined on a couch on his own, with Lucus's couch pushed up close to him. At the end of the group, was Hilaron's couch, where he sat more than lay. His nervousness was obvious, which seemed satisfying to David, because he himself was very merry. But if he had looked, then David would have seen that Lucus was pale, and he may have wondered why. But of course he was not a man who considered others' emotions much.

I had been given a couch below Lucus, at the end of the family group and opposite the younger of the cousins. Also at that end were Hilaron's elderly uncle, Matthias, and two of his middle-aged sons. With me they made up the lower section of the seating and completed the rectangular arrangement.

It had been obvious from the moment he arrived that Matthias was only there for duty sake and had no liking for David. He and his sons made their speeches of congratulation and looked warily at David and Hilaron and refused more than a few cups of wine, making it clear that they would have to leave early and could not stay the night.

By contrast, when the five young male guests, all cousins, of each other—not Hilaron, had arrived together, they had been in high spirits. They had heartily greeted Hilaron, embracing him roughly and then greeting everyone else present, and heaping them all with praise and the god's wishes for their health and good fortune. Then when they came to greet me, they had eyed me with surprise, yet approvingly, and made comment on my size and asked me where I came from.

They had obviously had wine before they arrived, and they laughed at my replies, which I made as if I was already filled with wine. David was also full of energy and excitement and laughed loudly with them. But it was obvious that everyone but he and the young men would have preferred to be somewhere else on that night, and Hilaron was pale and withdrawn, though he tried hard to act generously and as the guest of honor.

Once the final sweets had been served, Matthias and his sons made their farewells and left. And at this point the gathering became more raucous, and I saw one of the guests move his hand to his manhood and stroke it, and Lucus was leaning over and feeding David one of the small sweet balls of honey and nuts that remained on the table before him.

All evening one of the cousins, Yarron, the eldest, had been eyeing me off, and now he was reclining on his couch, looking at me with hooded, sex-filled eyes and making it clear he was hard by running his hand down over his robe to show the length and shape of his weapon as it lay up his belly. It was indeed a good size, and a small patch of dampness appeared to be forming on the white linen covering the rounded head of it.

I looked at David and said, sounding as if I had been drinking, "I have found your son Hilaron a most agreeable companion." And getting up I walked unsteadily up to Hilaron's couch, where I sat down by his stretched-out thighs. Hilaron was reclining back, turned to face me, and looked at me with some embarrassment and nervousness but also with lust in his eyes. I placed my hand on his bare calf and ran it up over his knee and up his thigh beneath his robe, stopping briefly to grope his swelling manhood and his big, young nuts, before running it on. I moved my hand up his flat belly and onto his chest, and his robe was now pushed up to reveal his growing manhood and his balls, as my fingers reached his right nipple and pinched it firmly and rolled it between my fingers. He whimpered quietly, and I leant in, parting his legs and lying between them as I kissed him on the lips.

Our tongues met inside his sweet mouth, and he lifted his legs up as we kissed, laying one over the back of the couch while the other he wrapped about my hips, his back arching as he rubbed his growing organ against my thigh and hip. Meanwhile, his hands tugged at my loincloth, pulling it off me so that my great weapon, already stiff, was free to swell and lengthen till it was soon hard and throbbing and moving against the soft silkiness of his thigh as his rubbed his own manhood up my belly.

I broke the kiss and looked about, seeing that David was sitting forward with his lips parted and his eyes hooded and had pulled Lucus between his legs, where he was on his knees and already swallowing David's weapon. And I knew that David was looking on his adult son, Hilaron, as just a highly desirable young man about to be taken by another. The cousins also looked on eagerly, Yarron now having his own weapon out from under his robe for all to see and running both hands up and down the slick shaft. And the other four young men were also working their own dicks, or each others', some exposed and some still hidden by their fine linen robes.

Moans came from several mouths, and Yarron cried out, "Show us if he can take that weapon of yours, Konan. I am eager to see if such a huge, thick pole truly can be driven into the tight hole he has between those firm young ass cheeks of his."

Cries of, "Yes. Yes," came from his brothers and cousins, and David's eyes were now swimming in lust as Lucus sucked. His experienced mouth moving up and down over David's length while his hands guided Lucus's head, his fingers curled tightly in his stepson's hair.

I had lifted Hilaron's ass up and now had both hands to his butt, with my thumbs pressed in at either side of his entrance, parting it. A lovely sight—to which I added two fingers, and he cried out as I entered his channel with them. I only withdrew my fingers to replace them with the head of my weapon. Working those fingers into his hole had opened him, as he had tightened up already after our afternoon's joinings.

"I will show you what can be achieved with patience," I said, my fingers now well in and Hilaron moaning as I rubbed them over his spot and he leaked juice from the slit in the bulbous head of his manhood.

"I want to try him too," Yarron cried, as I once more guided the head of my throbbing weapon to the entrance of one of the nicest asses I had plowed for some time. Hilaron whimpered and cried out as I worked myself into him, while he wriggled his butt and widened his legs to ease my entry.

I looked about to see two of the cousins now lying on one couch, both head to ass, and each sucking the other as their hands explored each other's asses. And David's head was now rolling back as he tugged Lucus's head rapidly back and forth, obviously near his spouting. And as David came I bottomed in his son and began a long, deep fucking of him, the pleasure of which was greatly increased by the sight of the activities being enjoyed by every other man in the room.

When David had filled Lucus's throat with his seed, he lay back spent, also watching and enjoying the activity, not noticing Lucus leave the hall briefly and return with a handful of plaited leather cords.

I continued to plow Hilaron, but now moving my weapon about inside him to gain maximum pleasure from his tight passage; then I withdrew my organ, a throbbing shaft standing up and leaking. And I turned to David.

His eyelids were hooded and his mouth was partly open as he looked at what I had to offer, and I saw that his hand was back on his own manhood, which was beginning to stiffen again.

"I have had the son," I said loudly, and moved toward David, "and enjoyed him well. And now I shall try the father."

David did not take in what I had said and remained reclining back on his couch, stroking himself, while the room became very quiet. I reached him and in a moment I had grasped his hips in my hands and was turning him over.

Finally he realized what was happening and he struggled against me. But then he discovered what I had known before I moved toward him. "No. What . . . ? No. Stop what . . . ? Who has done this?" he shouted angrily. For Lucus had used the cords to hobble him, tying David's ankles together as he had sat back fisting his manhood. And now he was helpless, his fists hitting out at me, but he was unable to stand and fell about, unbalanced, as he struggled. "Stop this animal," David cried in a rage.

But Hilaron had stood up after pulling his sword from beneath the cushion on his couch, "Yarron, Goron, I know why my father asked you here. And how much gold he offered you to have you cause me to fall from the roof terrace in a drunken accident." Hilaron's voice cried out above the racket as he held his sword up for the unarmed guests to see, for their weapons were in a chest by the entrance door as was the custom. "Leave now, and you shall have the promised gold still. I am the master of this house, and after tonight my grandfather's gold shall be mine as custom demands."

As Hilaron spoke I had turned David and trapped his thighs between mine. And I had hold of his wrists and forced his arms up above his head and his hands together. And though he trembled, Lucus found the courage to tie his wrists together even as David cursed and spat at him.

"You ungrateful bastard," David cried at Lucus. "Stop this. You are mine. I have treated you well. Stop this mad barbarian from . . ."

"You did not treat me well," Lucus cried, as he knotted the cords tightly, but still trembling and partly afraid of his stepfather. "You have treated me badly. Always."

Then, "Nooooo. . . , nooooooo. . . ," was all David could cry out as I forced my entry to his channel. It was indeed tight, and I doubted any man had been there before me. Or would be after me, so I made good use of the tightness, and after I finally had my balls pressed to his ass, I began a slow, deep plowing of him.

Hilaron's father whimpered and moaned loudly and lurched occasionally and tried to part his thighs to ease the pain he felt, but I liked the way his channel encased me and held him firmly.

The cousins had talked briefly among themselves; then Yarron spoke. "Gold is gold, and you have more right to it than your father ever had, Hilaron," he said. "But we want it tonight before we leave this house. A man can have a short memory of the promises he makes once a danger is past."

"So be it," Hilaron replied. "But a man is also a fool to have those recently plotting against him free in his own house and able to change their minds. So, if you are willing to be tied up and watched till morning, you may have your gold before you leave."

Yarron frowned at this and the others raised objections. "You may hold them hostage in some safe place till morning," He said, "But I shall remain free."

"What . . . ?" "No, Yarron, brother, no . . . ," his companions cried.

"That is the way of it," he said loudly to them. "No arguments."

Hilaron ordered his father's stepson, Lucus, to bind the four young men's wrists and ankles. And though they grumbled, Yarron silenced them and watched me taking David more than he bothered with his family. And, "My turn next," he said, as he moved closer to us.

I finally came then, throwing my head back and roaring as I filled David's passage with my seed. When I had withdrawn, Yarron moved up, and taking my place, entered David even more roughly than I had, with obvious enjoyment.

Meanwhile, I pulled Hilaron to me, "No," he said, "we cannot leave them here unguarded." But he didn't pull away from me.

"Pay them now," I said to him, "and let them take David with them, then bar the gates."

"But, the gold is not mine until the morning," he said firmly.

"Then you will have to guard them all night," I replied. "And you cannot do it alone."

"I shall watch them with you," Lucus said, from where he sat watching Yarron roughly plow the man who had so often taken him roughly. "I am glad that I am free of him at last," he said, " and I will make sure he cannot escape. Trust me Hilaron."

David was left tied and fucked repeatedly by Yarron throughout the night.

When dawn broke, the cousins were freed and Hilaron gave them the gold his father, David, had promised them if they had killed Hilaron in an accident during the night. They left happy, taking David, who was begging not to be taken away by Yarron, saying they would leave him at the crossroads.

Once they had gone, Hilaron was almost asleep. But after the gates into the courtyard had been barred behind the departing guests, he assembled the servants and stood before them, tired but proud.

"I am the master here now," he said in a loud, clear voice. "I am of age and have spent a night here as required, and now my father is gone back to his own property. Take heed now of what I say, for I will be a firm but caring master to those who work hard and are loyal to me. But for others, there will be no place for you in this house."

The old cook, Miriam, stood behind the other servants and tears flowed down her face at the news of Hilaron's inheritance, and she was unable to speak.

And when Hilaron had spoken, I put my arm about his shoulders and led him away, back to his bed, and I called Lucus to join us. Shortly after we slept, I admit, for it had been a long and tiring night—but not before I had worked my cock into Hilaron's ass to nestle there while I slept, so I could wake with it full, and hard, inside that sweet channel.

David still owned the farm that had been Lucus's mother's and there was nothing that could be done about that, so Lucus remained. I stayed on at the farmhouse for only the number of days it took to feel I had fed well and rested—and taken all the pleasure I wanted from the two willing men.

Then I was restless and the road to the east beckoned me, and I left the farmhouse early one morning, farewelled by the two contented men, and the household servants, as an honored guest should be. I took the road toward Persepolis after being given a farewell very different from my arrival at Hilaron's farm.

And as I followed the track from the farmhouse back up to the road I did not look back, but I wondered if it had been the gods, or chance, who had directed me to that farmhouse half a moon before.

I found the road was busy and I strode off toward the east and the fine city of Persepolis, easily passing the slow moving carts of wealthy merchants and the donkeys of poorer merchants who traveled with all their wares hanging from their saddles.

To be continued

Konan's journey through the ancient world continues in:

BARBARIAN TALES - BOOK FOUR

Road to Persepolis

Sabb

Once an accountant and sometime property developer, Sabb is a wild barbarian at heart, who knows that love is out there of you want to find it.

BOOKS BY SABB
The Legend of Holleystone Grange
Surprise Encounters
She is He
Wrong Man
Loyal to his King
Barbarian Tales - Book One - Traveler's Tales
Barbarian Tales - Book Two - Journeys Begin
Barbarian Tales - Book Three - The Inheritance
Barbarian Tales - Book Four - Road to Persepolis

www.barbarianspy.com

www.ingramcontent.com/pod-product-compliance
Lightning Source LLC
Chambersburg PA
CBHW020437180626
46812CB00003B/1283